SARA'S GOOD-BYE

Alec smiled at her. "We're all going to miss you around here."

"No one is going to miss anyone if that train leaves before we get there," Hetty interrupted abruptly.

Alec put his arm around Sara and led her to the buggy, but Sara broke away and ran back to hug her aunt Olivia.

"Oh, Aunt Olivia . . ." she whispered, as close to tears as she dared.

Olivia held her. "You take care . . . give your father our regards . . . you'll come back and visit . . . you're part of our family now."

"I won't forget," said Sara. She pulled herself away and allowed her uncle Alec to lift her into the buggy.

The family waved and shouted their good-byes from the porch as the buggy pulled away.

"Good-bye, dear!" called Janet, her handkerchief held to her face.

Sara turned and watched Rose Cottage and her family as they got smaller and smaller and finally disappeared behind the brow of the hill.

"Good-bye . . ."

Also available in the Road to Avonlea series from Bantam Skylark Books

Sara's Homecoming

Storybook written by

Heather Conkie

Based on the Sullivan Films Production
adapted from the novels of

Lucy Maud Montgomery

A BANTAM SKYLARK BOOK
NEW YORK · TORONTO · LONDON · SYDNEY · AUCKLAND

*Based on the Sullivan Films Production produced by Sullivan Films Inc.
in association with CBC and the Disney Channel with the participation of
Telefilm Canada adapted from Lucy Maud Montgomery's novels.*

*Teleplay written by Heather Conkie.
Copyright © 1991 by Sullivan Films Distribution, Inc.*

*This edition contains the complete text
of the original edition.*
NOT ONE WORD HAS BEEN OMITTED.

RL 6. 008–012

SARA'S HOMECOMING

*A Bantam Skylark Book / published by arrangement with
HarperCollins Publishers Ltd.*

PUBLISHING HISTORY
HarperCollins edition published 1992
Bantam edition / March 1993

ROAD TO AVONLEA *is the trademark of Sullivan Films Inc.*

*Skylark Books is a registered trademark of Bantam Books,
a division of Bantam Doubleday Dell Publishing Group, Inc.
Registered in U.S. Patent and Trademark Office and elsewhere.*

ISBN 0-553-48038-3

Chapter One

It was a quiet, lazy June day in the small village of Avonlea. The air was warm and soft as a blanket, and so still that no trace of the salt sea mingled with the scent of the early summer flowers that lined the picket fences.

The villagers went about their daily business. For many who greeted each other, the weather was the main topic of conversation. The older folks complained about the excessive heat and the young savored the promise of a long, hot summer. Even the horses seemed to be taking their time as they pulled buggies and carts along the main street, the clip-clopping of their hooves on the red dirt of the road the only sound breaking the silence.

Well, not quite the only sound. From the direction of the general store came the unmistakable rumble of intermittent snoring. Mrs. Biggins, who was trading news and gossip with Mrs. Spencer at her boarding house gate, glanced towards the source. Mrs. Spencer followed her gaze, and they both tittered behind their gloved hands. There on the porch, on a chair tilted back against the store wall, was Abner Jeffries, the official Chief Constable of Avonlea. At this moment, he wasn't looking out for the good people of Avonlea at all, officially or otherwise; his mouth was wide open in mid-snore.

If Mrs. Biggins and Mrs. Spencer had been any closer to the sleeping constable, they would have witnessed a feather floating gracefully downwards towards the man's nose. Just before it was about to reach its intended target, a hand reached out and caught it. A ten-year-old boy with tousled hair and a mischievous light in his eyes stared transfixed as, time after time, he dropped the feather over the sleeping Abner's nose. Felix King felt the undeniable thrill of tempting fate. He looked around to see if anyone was watching him, but his older sister Felicity and his cousin Sara Stanley were standing with their backs to him, reading the notice board in front of the store.

He picked up the feather from where it had fallen on the porch floorboards and once again let it float downwards towards the sleeping constable. Felix's eyes widened in delight as this time the feather missed its target entirely and instead approached Abner's cavernous mouth. He watched in fascination as the feather came to rest on Abner's tongue and, with one resounding snore, was whisked away into Abner's mouth, gone forever.

The screen door of the general store opened suddenly and slammed shut, causing Felix to jump guiltily aside. His father, Alec King, and Mr. Lawson, the proprietor, were carrying boxes of fireworks out to the front porch. Luckily for Felix, they were too busy to notice his look of relief at not being caught.

"I'll bet Avonlea will give even Charlottetown a run for their money as far as Dominion Day fireworks go," Mr. Lawson was saying, as he wiped his brow. "Thanks for your help, Alec."

"Don't mention it," replied Alec, as he added his box to the display of brightly colored fireworks.

Mr. Lawson straightened up, one hand rubbing his aching back.

"I'll get that flour for you too, Alec, while you're here!"

"Fine! I'll give you a hand," said Alec, and both men went back into the store.

Felix gave Abner Jeffries a backward glance, amazed that he still had not woken up, even with the door banging shut right beside him. Chuckling and shaking his head with glee, he sauntered over to inspect the fireworks.

Felicity and Sara were still busy looking at the notice board. A colorful poster featuring a dancing bear and a grinning clown advertised a coming circus.

"This is going to be the best Dominion Day ever," said fourteen-year-old Felicity King. "All these fireworks, and then just ten days from now, right here in Avonlea, a circus!"

"I can't wait!" said Sara, her cheeks flushed with excitement. The future looked bright. Summer stretched out ahead of her. School was out! And now, a circus to look forward to.

Felix's attention was drawn to the contents of one of the display boxes. "Look! Cracker-bangers! Great!" Felix swooped down on the box, but the store's screen door opened once again and slammed shut with a bang.

"Uh-uh! Put that back, Felix. You know you're not old enough to handle fireworks," his father warned.

Felix grudgingly put the bright-red cracker-banger back in its box and, turning his back, pretended to be wonderfully interested in a broken step on the porch of the general store. He knew that if he looked over he'd see the superior smiles of his sister and cousin.

Alec turned to accept the large bag of flour that Mr. Lawson handed to him. At the same time, Mr. Lawson leaned forward conspiratorially. "Alec," he said quietly, "Jeb Sloane is out behind the blacksmith's shop."

Alec looked sideways at Felicity, who was still engrossed in the circus advertisement, and Sara, who was tidying the piles of apples in the bushel baskets on the porch.

"Really?"

Mr. Lawson nodded. "He's taking bets on the Saturday race in Summerside."

"Uh huh," said Alec, busying himself with the bag of flour, which refused to stay upright in the back of the buggy. He piled some straw around it.

"Care to place any?" continued Mr. Lawson, in a whisper.

"Well, that depends," said Alec.

"On what?" asked Mr. Lawson.

Alec turned, his dark eyes twinkling. "On whether your wife's nearby. Elvira would tar and feather us if she caught us."

Mr. Lawson nodded knowingly with a small smile. "Well, she just happens to be away for a bit."

Alec slapped him heartily on the back. "Well then, what are we waiting for?"

Mr. Lawson grinned broadly. "Right...I'll just..." He looked around and spotted Sara, still tidying his displays. "Uh, Sara! Could you mind things here for a few moments? Your uncle and I have some...some important business to attend to."

Sara beamed. "Of course, Mr. Lawson. I'd be happy to take on the responsibility."

Felicity looked over her shoulder at Sara and rolled her eyes with obvious jealousy. With a toss of her brown curls, she walked away.

"Thank you!" said Mr. Lawson. "Alec, I've got a tip on a horse called Sea Wind," he said earnestly under his breath as they headed in the direction of the blacksmith's shop.

Sara straightened her shoulders and, with a proprietary smile, walked towards the entrance of the general store. *Her* general store. For the time being, anyway.

Felix watched his cousin with a wicked look in his eye. He snatched a cracker-banger from its box and handed two pennies to Sara as she walked by.

"Here's two cents for one cracker-banger," he said with a devilish smile.

Sara instantly handed him back his pennies. "No, Felix. Your father said you're not allowed to have any. Give it to me!" She said it in her best schoolteacher voice, the one she had heard her Aunt Hetty use so often, especially on Felix. But this time it did not seem to have the desired effect. Felix threw the pennies right back at her and took a match from his pocket.

"I've paid my money. I can take what I want," he retorted.

"Felix!" Exasperated, Sara tried to grab the cracker-banger and the match from her cousin.

Felix looked at the still-sleeping Abner Jeffries with a twinkle in his eye. "This'll wake him up!" he said, chuckling.

Once again, Sara attempted to retrieve the offending items from Felix, but he held them both beyond her reach.

"Felix! You're going to get me into trouble," said a frantic Sara.

"Oh, we wouldn't want Miss Goody-Goody to get in trouble, would we?" Felicity piped up from where she was perched decorously on her father's buggy.

With a final effort, just as Felix lit the match, Sara grabbed it from his hand and, with a flourish, tossed it over his shoulder into a barrel near the door.

"Mr. Lawson put me in charge, Felix. If you don't behave yourself I'll have to..."

Sara didn't have a chance to speak another word, for at that moment there was an explosion of sound and color and light from the barrel next to the door. Sara had unwittingly thrown the lit match into a barrel full of fireworks! All hell broke loose. Fireworks of every size and shape went off in all directions. A dazzling, rainbow-colored chain reaction began as sparks from one box set off all the others.

Felix watched with delight, his eyes as wide as saucers. Sara was horrified. She stood next to him, white-faced, hardly comprehending what she had done.

The cacophony was finally sufficient to wake the sleeping Abner Jeffries. He jumped to his feet just in time to see a Roman candle whiz by his nose. "What the devil...?" he exclaimed, watching in utter disbelief as it landed with a loud, whistling hiss and a shower of bright gold stars on the King buggy.

The poor horse reared and strained at its tether. Felicity, sitting in the buggy, let out a scream as she jumped to her feet. Unfortunately, the buggy was full of hay and straw, and it immediately went up in flames. Felicity, with unusual presence of mind, grabbed the nearest thing to her—an old potato sack—and leapt about, beating at the fire, trying in vain to put it out.

"Quick!" shouted Abner. "Unhitch the horses! Ring the fire bell! Whoa!" As he and Felix tried to unhitch the terrified horse, another horrific bang caused it to rear frantically. Abner tenaciously held onto its reins, hopping about crazily, keeping in mind the safety of his own toes. The horse bucked and neighed as a beautiful shower of silver and blue sparks floated down like snow.

Sara stood frozen for a second. Then, springing into action, she ran to the fire bell at the side of the store and pulled its rope frantically. The bell clanged as more fireworks exploded.

"Felix! Get some water!" yelled Felicity, still whacking at the fire in the buggy, but another exploding Roman candle proved too much for the poor horse, and, completely spooked, it tore itself from Abner and Felix's grasp and bolted down the street, buggy and all. Felicity went flying. She landed safely but unceremoniously in the horse's water trough.

Alec and Mr. Lawson ran from the direction of the blacksmith's shop just in time to see the horse heading straight for Mrs. Biggins and Mrs. Spencer, who were still standing, dumbstruck, mouths agape, at the boarding house fence.

"My store!" said Mr. Lawson, faintly.

Alec ran for the horse, but it was too late. The two ladies screamed and dove over the gate at the last minute to avoid being trampled. The wheels of the burning buggy caught Mrs. Biggins's immaculate picket fence and dragged it along behind it down the road.

Alec ran down the street after the horse and buggy as people flew in every direction to avoid the runaway.

Mr. Lawson stood in shocked silence, tugging at his hair as though he might just pull it out by the roots. "Look out! Get out of there! She's going to blow!" he finally blurted as rocket after rocket exploded. The others ran to join him just as one of the sparks landed in the barrel of cracker-bangers and created a grand finale of sparks, sizzles and explosions.

A fascinated crowd formed in a ring around the general store. When the din had subsided slightly, Mr. Lawson turned to the children, helplessly.

"My store!" he managed to squeak. "What…when…who…? Who is responsible?"

Felix and Felicity both turned and pointed at Sara.

"Sara…?" said Mr. Lawson weakly as Alec reappeared, disheveled and out of breath, but holding on to the still-quivering horse.

Sara was so upset she could barely speak. "Mr. Lawson…I'm…I'm sorry…I just don't know how this could have happened! I was trying to stop Felix from lighting a cracker-banger, and I guess…the box caught fire…I didn't mean it….Oh, Mr. Lawson, I just don't know how this could have happened!"

Another explosion ripped through the air, and Mr. Lawson ran towards his beloved store.

"My store! My store!"

Sara turned accusingly to Felix. "Felix, how could you?" she cried. "It was your…" But Felix wasn't paying any attention to her. He was still watching the fireworks display with delight.

When she looked to her Uncle Alec, she saw disappointment in his eyes.

Chapter Two

"Sara Stanley! Between the fireworks and that horse running wild, you're just lucky that no one was seriously hurt! As it is, I've got to replace that fence at the boarding house, and my buggy is completely destroyed! You know, young lady, if I was your father, I'd give you a darn good spanking!"

Alec King rarely lost his temper, but now, standing in the hallway at Rose Cottage, he was coming as close to it as anyone had ever seen. Felicity, soaked to the skin and wrapped in a blanket, stood smugly beside her father. Felix watched from the staircase, his face radiating innocence.

Sara stood silently, eyes glued to the floor, thoroughly ashamed. She adored her Uncle Alec, and for him to be this upset and angry with her was devastating.

"Worst of all, there won't be a single firework on Dominion Day," pouted Felicity.

"And it's all Sara's fault!" said Felix.

Sara had bitten her tongue many times on the trip from the village to Rose Cottage, but this was more than she could bear.

"It is not, Felix! You know perfectly well if you hadn't…"

"That will be enough, Sara," interrupted her Aunt Hetty, who had listened impassively to her brother Alec's charges. "Now go to your room."

Sara's Aunt Olivia gave Sara a quick look of sympathy but did not dare interfere.

"But Felix was the one that—" Sara began to protest.

"Go!" said Hetty sternly, pointing to the stairs. "Straight upstairs, I said, and not another syllable."

Sara's eyes flashed with anger at the injustice of it all, but she stuck her chin out and, without another word, she went up the stairs, her head held high.

Hetty turned and looked at her younger brother as if he were a pupil in her class at the Avonlea school. "Alec, when you've calmed down a bit, perhaps we can talk sensibly about all this…alone." Hetty looked at the children and then back at Alec.

"All right," he replied, getting her point. "But Sara has got to take responsibility for her actions. And if you don't see that she does, I will!"

Alec turned and slammed out the door, followed by Felix and Felicity, who were making little effort to hide their smugness.

As their footsteps faded away, Olivia King looked fearfully at her older sister. Poor Sara, she thought. Hetty must be furious with her. But to Olivia's surprise, Hetty turned from the door with a small chuckle.

"Fireworks indeed!"

The two sisters exchanged glances and smiled, Olivia with relief and Hetty with amusement.

"It's just like something Ruth would have done," said Hetty. Ruth was Sara's mother and Hetty and Olivia's beloved sister.

Hetty shook her head and sighed. She picked up a letter from the hall table.

"Well, I suppose the little culprit might at least be allowed to receive her mail."

Sara lay on her bed, staring malevolently at the ceiling. The brightly colored cabbage roses on her wallpaper and the soft breeze blowing through her white lace curtains could do nothing to cheer her up. Not in months had she felt so thoroughly alone and misunderstood. Tears of self-pity welled up in her eyes. Her own cousins, betraying her like that. She'd thought they liked her. In the months since she had arrived in Avonlea, she had gradually come to feel at home on the Island and with her relatives. It had not been easy, but she had sincerely believed that she'd reached the point, especially with Felicity, where they were more than just cousins, more than just mere relations that you were required to get along with. She thought they had become friends. She knew now that she must have been wrong. No friend would have acted as Felicity did that afternoon. It just wasn't fair!

Whenever she felt down in the dumps, Sara's mind turned to thoughts of her father, so far away in Montreal. How she missed him. It seemed so long since she had seen him.

Her thoughts were interrupted by a brisk knock on her door. Sara rolled her eyes and readied herself for the lecture that was sure to come.

Aunt Hetty knocked again and entered, her face an inscrutable mask. She lost no time in launching into a diatribe.

"Sara Stanley, it never ceases to amaze me what unbelievably ridiculous scrapes you manage to get yourself into!"

Sara turned and faced her aunt, looking imploringly into her eyes.

"Aunt Hetty, it wasn't my fault...not all of it."

Hetty was having none of that. "Least said, soonest mended," she said, in her best schoolmarm tone. Then she took out a letter from behind her back and held it out to Sara, with a hint of a smile. "This arrived for you this afternoon."

Sara's face was transformed! "Papa!" she breathed as she ripped open the envelope and took out its contents.

Hetty peered over her shoulder as Sara began to read. Sara looked pointedly at her aunt and tipped the letter to prevent her from seeing it. Hetty raised an eyebrow and reluctantly left her niece to her privacy.

The kitchen at Rose Cottage was filled with the scent of freshly baked bread and rolls, and Olivia was just taking the last loaf out of the oven when Hetty entered the room. Hetty shook her head and sat down at the table. Olivia smiled and sat down next to her older sister. They were a study in contrasts. Hetty's hair was gathered severely on top of her head, not a strand out of place. Her white, high-necked blouse, with its cameo brooch, was immaculate and tucked in smartly to a dark-purple wool gabardine skirt. She hadn't an ounce of spare flesh on her erect frame, and people often thought she was taller than she actually was. Olivia, on the other hand, was soft and blossomy. Her dark hair fell in gentle, natural waves, always threatening to come out of its prison of pins and combs. The two exchanged a glance.

"You're exactly right, Hetty. It is just like something Ruth would have done," said Olivia with an amused smile.

Hetty chuckled. "I always said a lit firecracker would be the only way to get Abner Jeffries moving."

Olivia giggled, but a sound in the kitchen doorway made them both turn around. Sara stood there, her letter still clutched in her hand. Hetty immediately put on her serious face.

"I don't believe I gave you permission to leave your room, young lady," she began, but something in Sara's expression stopped her.

"Papa wants me to come home."

It was a simple statement, but all that it implied filled the room with an expectant silence. Olivia caught her breath and bit her bottom lip.

Hetty's mouth trembled slightly and pursed into what she hoped was an encouraging smile. "Oh…?" she managed to utter, patting an imaginary errant hair into place.

"I think it's best…I mean…I'm sure you will agree, it's time I went back to Montreal." Sara's voice echoed all of her pent-up hurt and humiliation.

"Oh Sara…" began Olivia, but Hetty cautioned her with a sharp glance.

"Well…I suppose you were bound to sooner or later, but I hate to see you go back under the…present circumstances."

Surely there was a way to handle this, some way that she could change Sara's mind without appearing to do so.

Sara said nothing. Hetty threw a hopeful look at Olivia and decided that the role of devil's advocate might be the best one to employ. Certainly it had worked for her at the school, on both pupils and parents.

"Well, if you're sure that's what you want…" She paused, hoping that Sara would fill the space with a denial. But Sara stood silent and pale in front of them, her expression fixed and resolved. It was obvious that she had already made up her mind.

"So...you're determined to go," said Hetty quietly.

Sara nodded.

"Then I'll accompany you. To see you get there safely," said Hetty matter-of-factly, trying to hide her hurt.

"You needn't bother," said Sara, her chin held high. "I'll be fine on my own."

Chapter Three

Early-morning shadows traveled along the porch of Rose Cottage and among the tangle of roses entwined on the gingerbread trim. The sun had barely made itself visible on the horizon, but the lamps inside the house were lit. Hetty and Olivia King's hired boy, Peter Craig, appeared from the direction of the back shed, leading a horse. He walked as if in his sleep, head down, trudging forward, one foot in front of the other, until he reached the buggy, already stationed out front. He woke up with a start to the sound of the slamming screen door and Hetty's voice.

"Haven't you hitched up the buggy yet, Peter Craig?" she demanded, coming down the porch steps in a flap, carrying several bags, dressed in her traveling clothes. "We'll miss the blasted train at this rate!" She looked with disgust at the still unhitched buggy. "You put the bags in. I'll do this!" She grabbed the reins from his hands. "When you want something done right, you have to do it yourself," she mumbled to herself.

Peter shook his head and rubbed his eyes. This was the way things had been now for the last few days. Everything was turned upside-down. Tempers flared one moment, tears were shed the next. No one was speaking to anyone else. Sara had refused to see her cousins, and the grown-ups weren't any better. Alec and Hetty were barely on nodding terms. He, for one, would be glad to see things get back to normal. He wasn't sure if they ever would. But he was sure of one thing: he was certainly going to miss Sara.

Olivia appeared on the porch, dabbing at her eyes. She looked as tired as he felt, Peter thought to himself. Aware of Hetty's eyes stabbing him in the back, he started to load the bags into the buggy.

"Oh, Hetty," said Olivia in a broken voice, "it all seems so sudden. I hate her to have to go without having a chance to patch things up."

"I told you, Olivia," said Hetty. "She was bound to go back sooner or later. If that's what she wants, the best that I can do is to make sure she gets there safely." Hetty was always at her most brusque when she didn't believe a word that she uttered.

Olivia bit her lip, but the tears started flowing once again.

"There will be no tearful farewells this morning, Olivia King! It will just upset matters." Hetty straightened up from successfully hitching the horse to the buggy and brushed her hands together.

Sara appeared beside Olivia on the porch with two more bags in her hands. She was beautifully dressed in a cream-colored traveling coat and a hat trimmed with navy-blue ribbons.

Hetty looked at Sara's bags to avoid meeting the child's eyes.

"Goodness knows why you had to empty your closets, Sara. It isn't as if you'll never visit." Her voice wavered and threatened to give her away, but the moment was interrupted by the sound of buggy wheels approaching from the direction of the King farm.

Hetty whirled around and looked down the

road. Appearing out of the early-morning mist was a horse and buggy. Alec held the reins, and with him were Janet, Felix, Andrew, Felicity and Cecily.

"Oh, good Lord!" Hetty muttered under her breath.

Olivia, with her arm around Sara, walked down the steps of the porch to greet them, desperately trying not to cry.

"Morning, Hetty," said Alec evenly, hopping down and giving his hand to Janet.

Hetty did not move forward to welcome them. She stood stubbornly still, with her hands on her hips.

"Alec, I thought I told you we were going to make this departure as swift and easy as possible."

Janet paid her no heed and hugged Sara to her ample bosom, trying not to cry. "Now, Sara dear," she said, "you take care of yourself, and come back for a visit as soon as you can, do you hear me?"

The children hung back, all except little Cecily, who joined her mother and hugged Sara as if she might never let go.

"I don't want you to go, Sara," she sobbed, her face buried in Sara's arm.

For the first time, Sara wavered as she hugged her youngest cousin.

"Please, don't cry, Cecily. It's all right."

Janet motioned to the older children, who hung back self-consciously.

"Say goodbye…Felicity…Felix…"

Andrew came forward and stiffly extended his hand to Sara.

"Have a good trip…"

"I'll write to you," replied Sara, equally stiff.

Felix and Felicity were still standoffish, and Sara refused to give an inch.

Janet urged them on. "Felix, say goodbye. Felicity…"

Sara looked deliberately past them with a controlled, angry expression. Felicity came forward.

"Goodbye, Sara…" she said, hesitating.

"Goodbye…" replied Sara, hoping that Felicity would say more. When she didn't, Sara painted the stony look on her face once again.

Janet pushed Felix forward and he dug his toe into the dirt. He knew he should say something—he'd been wanting to for days—but…

"Bye Sara…I'm, uh…well, you know…"

Sara ignored him and started to walk to the buggy. Her Uncle Alec fell into step beside her.

"Sara, the buggy's good as new now. I just

had to replace a few boards in it. I'm sorry
I...lost my temper."

Sara stopped and looked up at him. She
shrugged her shoulders. "It's all right..." she
replied. She wanted to hug him, to tell him the
truth—that she never meant to cause any harm,
that it was all a misunderstanding, that she
wished she could turn back the clock and make
everything all right again. But she didn't. She
couldn't. The Kings had their full share of stub-
born pride, but the Stanleys had invented it.

Alec smiled at her, but the twinkle was miss-
ing from his eyes. "Well, you'll be back for a visit
soon, I hope," he said, his voice becoming gruff.
"We're all going to miss you around here."

"No one is going to miss anyone if that train
leaves before we get there," Hetty interrupted
abruptly.

Alec put his arm around Sara and led her to
the buggy, but Sara broke away and ran back to
hug her Aunt Olivia.

"Oh, Aunt Olivia..." she whispered, as close
to tears as she dared.

Olivia held her. "You take care...give your
father our regards...you'll come back and
visit...you're part of our family now...remem-
ber that..."

"I won't forget," said Sara.

"Oh Sara, I'll miss you so much," said Olivia, and her tears came freely at last.

Sara pulled herself away and allowed her Uncle Alec to lift her into the buggy. She sat beside Peter in the driver's seat, and Alec helped Hetty up in turn.

"Giddyup!" called Peter, as he flicked the reins and the horse started forward.

The family waved and shouted their good-byes from the porch as the buggy pulled away.

"Goodbye, dear!" called Janet, her handker-chief held to her face.

Olivia was still crying, and Alec put his arm around her.

Sara turned and watched Rose Cottage and her family as they got smaller and smaller and finally disappeared behind the brow of the hill.

"Goodbye..."

Chapter Four

At any other time and under any other cir-cumstances, the journey to the train station would have been beautiful. The waves rolled in and crashed upon the shore as the horse and buggy traveled along a winding road bordered by the sea on one side and another sea of daisies and cornflowers on the other. The sweet smell of clover hovered in the morning breeze, and the dew on the golden fields sparkled like diamonds.

By the side of the road, a sign was being erected advertising the arrival of the traveling circus. Just as they passed, the buggy lurched and rolled, acquiring a life of its own as it suddenly came unhitched.

"Miss King...I think something's wrong here," said Peter, with some trepidation. "How did you hitch up? Are you sure you did it right?" Peter held on for dear life to the horse's reins as the buggy swung wildly, but the horse was having none of this and, pulling the reins painfully through Peter's fingertips, it galloped off, straps and harnesses flying. The buggy rolled to a stop.

Hetty knew full well that, in her haste, she had probably hitched it up improperly, but she was certainly not going to let a hired boy get the best of her.

"If you'd done it in the first place as I told you to..." she complained, watching the horse as it galloped away.

"But you said..." stammered Peter.

"Never mind what I said," Hetty snapped.

"What are we going to do?" exclaimed Sara. "We'll miss the train!"

"I could chase after him," said Peter, jumping down from the buggy just as the horse disappeared around a bend in the road, heading back towards Rose Cottage.

"A fat lot of good that would do!" said Hetty. "You'd never catch him! God's nightgown! What are we going to do?"

As if in answer to a prayer, rumbling along behind them came a funeral buggy, draped in black crepe, its black horse bedecked and plumed. Hetty's eyes narrowed as she reviewed their options. Then, to Sara and Peter's surprise, she jumped nimbly from the buggy and flagged it down.

The driver was a wizened old man of indeterminate age who looked as if he might be a passenger in his own vehicle in the very near future. He looked down at Hetty with a scowl and a sneer.

"That your horse I seen go by?" he asked, and he spat out some tobacco at Hetty's feet.

"Yes," said Hetty.

"It come loose did it?"

"Can you drive us to the train station?" asked Hetty, annoyed at the man's statement of the obvious but realizing that he offered the only answer to their dilemma.

"Well now, happens I'm goin' in that direction."

Hetty looked back at Sara and Peter in triumph. "Put the bags in the back Peter." She paused and looked at the grizzly driver as a thought crossed her mind. "It is empty, isn't it?" she asked, nodding her head towards the coffin-shaped carriage.

The driver smiled wickedly, enjoying her discomfort.

"For the time bein'. I'm on a pick-up." He spat again for punctuation.

Hetty smiled wanly and motioned to the children, who were standing a safe distance from this carriage of death.

"Come along, Sara. Sit up next to the driver. Peter, the bags!"

Peter put the bags in the empty glass compartment unwillingly.

"It's bad luck, Miss King."

"The only bad luck around here is you, Peter Craig! Now go and find that horse or you'll be in real trouble!"

Hetty climbed up next to Sara and the old driver. With a snap of the reins, he drove away. Sara leaned out and waved.

"Goodbye, Peter!" she called.

Alone, in the middle of the red road, Peter waved back.

"Goodbye!"

Little did he know how often Sara would recall his words: "It's bad luck, Miss King."

Chapter Five

The carriage wheels flew over the cobblestone street. The horse's hooves clattered in rhythm. Noise surrounded them—the rattle of the wheels, the horns of the motor-cars, the whistles of people hailing cabs, the calls of the newspaper boys. Sara couldn't help smiling. She hadn't realized how much she had missed the hustle and bustle of her beloved Montreal. And soon she would see Papa!

Her Aunt Hetty clung to her arm as the carriage wheeled around a corner and entered the gates of a street lined with trees that sheltered gracious homes. Hetty was not smiling.

"No one to meet us! Trust Blair Stanley! How typical!! I made it perfectly clear what time our train would arrive!"

"But the train was early, Aunt Hetty!" Sara protested gently as the carriage pulled into the circular driveway of a huge stone house.

"Look! We're here! Aunt Hetty! We're home! This is our house!"

Hetty looked through the carriage window with undisguised amazement.

"Good Lord! It's the size of Buckingham Palace!"

By the time she had collected herself, Sara was already up the stone steps and throwing open the great carved wooden door. A fresh-faced girl in uniform appeared, a delighted smile on her face.

"Welcome home, Miss Sara!" she said, her voice lilting with a Scottish accent straight from the Highlands.

"Miss Sara!" said Hetty to herself. "A maid to answer the door, indeed!"

Hauling their suitcases, despite the pleas of the driver, Hetty followed Sara through the door, past the maid, and found herself in a huge vestibule. In the distance she could hear Sara calling, her voice echoing in the vastness of the hallway.

"Papa! We're here! Nanny Louisa!"

Hetty looked wide-eyed about her. Directly in front of her was a grand staircase that wound its way up to and past a stained-glass window, far superior even to the ones in the Avonlea church. Her gaze followed a row of oil paintings hanging side by side along the oak-paneled walls. She blushed and rolled her eyes at the statue of a naked Aphrodite that decorated the Stanley hall.

"How inappropriate," she thought to herself. "What sort of a place is this to raise a child?"

"May I help you with those?" The voice came from behind, close to her shoulder, startling her. Hetty closed her mouth abruptly, not wishing to appear the proverbial country cousin, and allowed the girl to take Sara's baggage from her hands.

Sara removed her gloves and hat and tossed them carelessly over Aphrodite's outstretched arm. Even though it was a great relief to see even part of the brazen alabaster figure modestly covered, Hetty could not stand slothfulness.

"Sara! Don't throw your clothes about," she instructed, glad to be on familiar ground, at least in one way, with Sara. But Sara paid her no heed and ran to the top of the staircase landing.

"Papa! Where are you? Nanny Louisa!"

A woman's voice came from the second floor.

"Sara! Sara my darling! Is that you?"

Hetty knew that voice. A steely feeling in the pit of her stomach reminded her of her first meeting with its owner, when Sara had first arrived, her nanny in tow, in Avonlea.

Nanny Louisa J. Banks appeared on the landing, framed in the magnificent, sun-drenched colors of the stained-glass window. She seemed smaller and grayer than Hetty remembered her. Sara raced to her and threw her arms around her.

"Nanny!"

"Oh my Sara! My little Sara! Is it really you? Glory! Glory!" The gray hair blended with the gold as they stood, embracing, oblivious to Hetty King's glare.

"I missed you!" Sara said over and over again. "It's so good to be back!"

"My dear little Sara. Safe home again," murmured Nanny Louisa, and then her soft eyes became the color of hard granite as she spotted Hetty King over Sara's head, standing as large as life in her downstairs foyer. She seemed smaller and less formidable than she remembered her.

Louisa J. Banks drew herself up to her full height of five-foot two and one-half inches and looked down on Hetty over her wire-rimmed glasses. Hetty stared right back at her, and instantly the old rivalry was picked up from where it had left off.

"Miss King." Nanny Louisa spoke crisply and primly, as though she were picking lint off her sweater.

"Miss Banks," returned Hetty, her voice controlled and wary.

Sara was oblivious to anything but the excitement of being home. She ran up the flight of stairs from the landing. "I have to see my room!" she tossed over her shoulder.

"Is your father getting the bags, Sara?" Nanny Louisa called after her. Sara didn't hear her, and she turned back to Hetty. "Well, where is Blair?"

"That's what we'd like to know," said Hetty stiffly. "We waited and waited at the station, but it became perfectly obvious that no one was coming to collect us. We had to make our own way."

Nanny Louisa looked puzzled. "How odd! He told me specifically not to send the chauffeur. I suppose he got caught up in his business. He's been rushed off his feet. He seems to be in three places at once these days."

"Everywhere but the train station," Hetty couldn't help but add.

Sara appeared at the top of the stairs once again, and before Hetty could say anything she threw one leg over the banister and slid down.

"Sara, stop that!" Hetty was flabbergasted and terrified at the same time. "You're going to break your neck! You are a young lady, not a barbarian."

Sara didn't answer; instead, she ran up to the top of the stairs and slid down the banister a second time.

"Nanny Louisa lets me, don't you Nanny Louisa?" she said breathlessly.

Nanny Louisa gave Hetty a "Don't-give-orders-under-my-roof!" look and said "It's perfectly safe."

Hetty, not one to let her position of authority be usurped, not even one little bit, retorted, "I'm glad you have finally realized, Miss Banks, that 'family' has more to say about discipline than 'hired help,'" she said, her voice thick with sarcasm.

Louisa J. Banks dismissed Hetty with a look and summoned the young maid, who waited by the front door, with a curt wave.

"Clearly you're overtired. I trust you will find your room adequate."

Sara ran past both of them up the stairs and once again disappeared.

The maid rushed forward and started to take hold of Hetty's bags and hat boxes. Hetty motioned her away.

"No...thank you. I'll manage." She followed Nanny Louisa's erect back up the stairs.

"It's small," Louisa was saying, "but I think you'll find it an improvement on the chicken coop I recall you once offered me. Besides, I don't suppose you will be staying long." She turned and faced Hetty defiantly.

Hetty narrowed her eyes. How like the woman to throw that old business about the chicken coop in her face. "I will be staying until I'm convinced that Sara's desire to return here is not merely a whim."

Nanny Louisa turned her back on Hetty and continued up the stairs. "Come along," was all she said.

Chapter Six

A beautiful, shiny black motor-car drew up into the circular driveway. When it came to a stop, a man in uniform hopped out of the driver's side and, with great dignity, walked around to the passenger side and opened the door. A very tall, handsome, dark-haired man seemed to unravel his long limbs to disembark.

"Thank you, Pierre. That will be all for today," he said as he crossed the driveway in two long strides, took the front steps in one and entered the house.

The maid fluttered around him as she took his hat and walking stick, but the man's eyes were on the small, blond figure that had just appeared at the top of the second-floor landing.

"Papa!"

Sara ran at top speed down the stairs and threw herself into his arms. Blair Stanley grinned and caught his daughter, swinging her around and around until she was quite dizzy.

"So here you are! Finally back! Safe and sound! I was worried sick! I couldn't find you at the station!"

A woman's dark figure appeared in front of the stained-glass window, watching them silently. Blair glanced up as she came down the stairs majestically.

"Hetty! Welcome to Montreal!" Blair reached his sister-in-law halfway down the stairs and embraced her warmly.

Hetty was quite taken aback by his forwardness. She had never really forgiven this man for taking away her youngest sister, and she still harbored the feeling that somehow he was to blame for her early death. The two of them came together only in their common love for Sara.

"And a fine welcome it was too, Blair," she said with icy coolness.

"Your train was early! You should have waited!" said Blair, still smiling.

Nanny Louisa appeared at the top of the stairs, but she held back, not wanting to interrupt Sara's reunion with her father.

"I told you, Aunt Hetty," said Sara, clinging to her father's hand.

"We waited quite long enough, thank you," retorted Hetty.

"Well, you're safely here now, and that's the main thing! Oh, it's good to have you back!" He gave Sara another hug and then held her away from him, marveling at how she had grown. How the pink in her cheeks became her. How she resembled her dear mother so incredibly.

"I missed you so much!" said Sara softly.

"I missed you too!" said Blair, and then he smiled a secretive smile. "Now, I have a little surprise for you, so why don't you—"

"A surprise! Papa, what is it?"

"Patience! Patience!" said Blair, teasing. "I'm sure you both want to freshen up. Why don't you go upstairs with Nanny Louisa and—"

Sara's father was interrupted by the sound of a small, discreet cough from the doorway. It was the maid, who was reluctant to disturb the master when he was so obviously happy to have his only daughter back.

"Excuse me, Mr. Stanley. There's a call for you from the warehouse," she said timidly.

Blair turned to her with impatience. "Tell them I'm unavailable! I've got more important business here!"

"They said it was urgent..." The maid's voice trailed off.

Blair sighed with resignation. "All right, all right...I'll take it." He gave Sara a little pat in the direction of the stairs. "You hurry back, young lady!"

Sara laughed and ran up the stairs to where Nanny Louisa waited. Hetty followed, looking daggers at Blair's back as he disappeared into the parlor to take his call.

"Surely you people can handle it on your own. My daughter has just arrived home ..."

Blair's brow was furrowed. Much as it pleased him to have built Stanley Imports back up from nothing, he knew that this accomplishment had carried its own price. From the day he had been unjustly accused of embezzling money from his own company and been placed under house arrest, he had had but three ambitions: to prove himself innocent, to rebuild the company back to its former stature, and, most important, to shield Sara from the unhappy situation at all costs. But now that it was all over, his most fervent desire was to have her home again with him, to catch up with her life and spend time with her. Now, he thought determinedly, if only his business interests would allow him the time to do so.

Sara entered the room and stood in the parlor doorway, her face shining, anticipating her surprise. But her father's tone of voice reached her.

"I realize that it requires my signature, but surely it can wait until tomorrow..." Blair sighed with frustration as the voice on the other end of the line droned on insistently. "All right," he finally said, "I'll be there as soon as I can. Goodbye."

He hung up the phone and turned to see Sara.

"You have to go out?" she asked quietly.

Blair forced a smile on his face. "I'm afraid so. But I won't be long. And I certainly won't keep you waiting for your surprise."

Sara brightened a bit, and Blair went over to a walnut armoire and opened one of its doors. He took out a beautifully beribboned and gift-wrapped box and handed it to her. Sara beamed and began to open it in a ladylike manner, delicately undoing the ribbons and paper, trying not to spoil them. The suspense was too great, however, and before long she was ripping it open with abandon, making her father laugh. Inside, under layers of pale laven-der tissue, was a beautiful blue dress, covered in ecru lace. Sara lifted it out and held it against herself in rapture. Never in all her life had she seen a dress as beautiful as this one. Then she looked down and realized there was something else in the box. There was a doll, with flaxen hair, just like Sara's, and she was wearing a miniature replica of the same beautiful blue lace dress.

"Oh Papa! It's beautiful! And I love her! Thank you."

Her father wrapped his arms around her again. She really did love her presents, but the most wonderful thing of all was to be home and hugging her father once again. She couldn't help thinking how silly the dress would look back home on the Island, and how Felix would laugh and call her doll "sissy." But that was P.E.I., and this was Montreal.

Blair reluctantly pulled himself away and looked at the gold watch pinned to his vest.

"Well, I'm sorry I have to leave you, but the sooner I go, the sooner I'll be finished. If everything goes well, I'll be back within the hour." He kissed Sara on the top of her head and, taking her by the arms, he looked directly into her blue eyes. Again, he was struck by how much she resembled Ruth. He swallowed hard, suddenly overcome by a tender but painful emotion.

"Tomorrow is your day. We'll pack a picnic and drive out to the country where no one can find us." He looked hard at her, as if fully realizing for the first time how much this child of his meant to him, how much he had missed her since she went away. "I love you, Sara."

"I love you too, Papa," said Sara, squeezing his hand.

Blair gave her a little wave and strode out of the room. Sara smiled and watched him go.

Chapter Seven

The moon was just beginning to appear over the tiled rooftops as Sara stared out her bedroom window to the street below. It was so different from the view from her window at Rose Cottage. There, when the moon was just coming up, she could faintly see its sparkle on the distant sea. The frogs would probably be singing by now, too, she thought. She smoothed down the lace on the front of her new dress. She had been determined to wear it for dinner that night, and had had quite a disagreement with Aunt Hetty about it. But now, with the dinner hour come and gone... She turned back to her doll.

"It's time you went to bed, Sara," said Hetty from where she sat, busily crocheting, perched on the velvet sofa in the little sitting room off Sara's bedroom.

"I want to wait for Papa," replied Sara, parting the heavy velvet drapes once again and looking out the window, listening for the purr of the motor-car.

"I feel like we've been waiting for your Papa all day long." Hetty couldn't help it; annoyance always crept into her voice whenever she spoke to or about Blair Stanley.

"He said he'd be back within the hour," said Sara.

"You're just going to have to get used to this, Sara, since this is what you so keenly desire. Living in *Montreal*." Hetty always pronounced the word Montreal as if it was Calcutta or Madagascar or some other country that she had only read about in books. "And you'd best get used to your father's heedless ways, my child," she continued. "And his busy schedule!"

The low chime of the distant doorbell floated through the air. Sara rushed from the room.

"Maybe that's him!"

The maid hurried across the hall from the direction of the kitchen to answer the door. And just when she had finally settled down to her own meal...she thought to herself. Who would be arriving at this time of night? The master always let himself in. She opened the door, and a gentleman bowed slightly to her.

"May I speak to Miss Louisa J. Banks, please?" he inquired politely and firmly.

"Why, yes. Please come in." The young girl was just about to call upstairs when Louisa emerged from the parlor.

"What is it, Mary?" she asked.

Sara appeared at the top of the stairs, with Hetty behind her.

"Miss Banks, Ma'am, this gentleman would like to speak with you," said Mary, giving a little bob.

Nanny Louisa came forward and extended her hand. "May I help you, Mr. ...?"

"Inspector Barwood of the Montreal police, Ma'am."

"Yes?" Her eyes questioned and her back stiffened.

The inspector glanced up to the top of the stairs, where Sara still stood. "Perhaps it would be advisable if the child..."

Nanny Louisa looked from the inspector's grave face to Sara, and then back again. "Mary, could you take Sara to her room, please..." she said, hardly recognizing her own voice.

Sara's face froze. A faint tingling in her forehead preceded a small, gnawing, raw ache in the pit of her stomach. Something was wrong. Mary came towards her up the stairs, but she was not going anywhere.

The inspector's voice droned on. "I regret to have to tell you that there has been an...accident at the Stanley Import warehouse."

"An accident?" repeated Nanny Louisa.

"Where's Papa?" said Sara, shrilly.

"Please, Mary. Take Sara—" said Louisa.

"Come along, Miss Sara…" said Mary softly. Sara fought her off. "No!"

"Nothing has happened to Mr. Stanley, has it?" Louisa was asking.

"I'm afraid so, Ma'am. Mr. Stanley was inspecting a shipment, apparently, and one of the second-story scaffolds collapsed."

He took Louisa Banks by the arm and gently led her to a chair, but she had no intention of sitting down. Getting up frantically, she demanded, "Which hospital is he in? We must go to him immediately!"

Once again, the man took her arm and eased her back into the chair.

"Ma'am, please. I'm afraid Mr. Stanley was killed instantly."

A ringing, buzzing noise filled Sara's ears. She wasn't hearing this. She couldn't be hearing this. And yet there was Nanny Louisa collapsed in shock in the chair in the hall. And the gasp behind her was from her Aunt Hetty, who instantly gathered her up in her arms. Mary, the maid, was starting to weep quietly, and now Nanny Louisa was coming towards her up the stairs, her face as gray as her hair. No! It wasn't happening. The buzzing grew louder. Then there was silence, and blackness.

Chapter Eight

People moved slowly, back and forth, in groups and alone. Their voices were hushed. Their dark clothes blended into the background of the black-draped cloth on which a coffin sat in the King Farm parlor. Sara stared at the waxen profile of her father. She could hear Aunt Hetty greeting people, thanking them for coming. Next to her stood Nanny Louisa. The events of the last week had aged her. It had been a fearful journey from Montreal. But there she stood, next to her arch-enemy, upright and proud. For once, in their grief, the two women were united.

Because Sara was so quiet, sitting by the coffin, outwardly composed, not shedding a tear, people seemed to forget she was there. For that, she was grateful. Shreds of conversation floated by her, through a thick fog, and reverberated in her ears.

"Poor child. First her mother, and now this."

"It's amazing to see a child so composed.

Why, Meggie Truby screamed and threw a blue fit when they carried her mother out. But then the Trubys are such a vulgar family." Sara recognized Mrs. Potts's voice.

"They say he was crushed," another, more elderly voice whispered.

"What a mercy that he died instantly..." That was Reverend Leonard.

The elderly voice continued relentlessly. "The funeral home did a wonderful job of laying him out. He looks so composed for someone who was—"

Sara could hear Reverend Leonard excuse himself before the woman could finish.

"—crushed...Reverend Leonard? Now why did he run away like that?"

Sara felt a hand on her shoulder and looked up. Her Aunt Janet, looking so unlike herself in a heavy, black silk dress, stood smiling sadly down at her.

"Can I get you anything, dear?"

Sara shook her head and managed to smile back. "No thank you, Aunt Janet," she said. Another hand lay gently on her other shoulder. She followed the arm up to the face—Reverend Leonard's face.

"He's at peace now, Sara."

What a strange thing to say, Sara thought, but she smiled at him as he passed.

Janet wanted to say more to Sara. She wanted to pull her out of that chair and hug her, but Mabel Sloane chose that moment to approach her, her plate filled with apple turnovers.

"Who made these turnovers, Janet? Did you?" she was asking, stuffing one of the pastries into her mouth.

Distracted, Janet drew her away from Sara.

"No…no, actually Felicity did."

What a ridiculous woman, she thought. Talking about turnovers at a time like this.

"They're delicious," continued Mabel. "Now please introduce me to that Banks woman. I've heard so much about her. You know how people talk…"

From directly behind her, Sara could hear what sounded like Mrs. Lawson's voice.

"Did you see the article in the Charlottetown paper? Sara! An heiress! Imagine."

"The Stanley crypt in Montreal is supposed to be as big as the royal family's," the same elderly voice added.

"It's fitting, though," came Aunt Janet's voice, "that Blair wanted to be buried next to dear Ruth."

Sara turned slightly to see her Aunt Olivia dab her eyes. Alec approached her with his arm around Felix and Felicity's shoulders. Andrew stayed in the background. It was obvious that neither Felicity nor Felix knew how they were supposed to act towards her. She wished fervently that she could somehow make it easier for them, but she felt frozen, incapable of anything but sitting quietly with her hands folded.

Felicity came forward, awkwardly. "How are you, Sara?"

"How do you think she is, Felicity?" said Felix, sarcastically.

Felicity's lower lip started to tremble, and tears appeared in her eyes. "I'm so sorry, Sara...I really am...I just don't know what to say to you."

Sara looked up at her. "Felicity, it's all right. You needn't say anything."

After another awkward moment of silence, Felix and Felicity melted away into the crowd, and Sara became aware that Alec had drawn up a chair next to her.

"How are you feeling?" he asked, his voice low and gentle.

For the first time in days, Sara felt something stirring deep inside her, something that, once allowed to the surface, would take over completely. She knew if she said even one word, whatever it was would win.

Alec cleared his throat. "Sara, if you ever need to talk, anytime...I just want you to know, you can confide in me. You're like one of my own children."

"No one can ever take my father's place, so please don't try, Uncle Alec." Sara heard the words come out of her mouth, but they sounded far away, as though someone else had said them.

Alec took a deep breath. He patted her arm and moved away. Sara wanted to scream, to hold on to him. But she couldn't. She could only sit and try to keep whatever was deep within her hidden away.

Hetty watched her niece from across the room, where she stood with Reverend Leonard. The man followed her gaze.

"Sara is being such a little soldier," he said.

Hetty shook her head slowly. She wasn't so sure as she watched Sara, hidden behind the coffin, leaning her cheek against it.

"Come ye blessed of my Father, inherit the Kingdom prepared for you from the foundation of the world. Grant this, we beseech thee,

O merciful Father, through Jesus Christ, our Mediator and Redeemer. Amen."

The funeral came to an end. A grim-looking group began to walk away from the newly dug grave, now heaped with flowers. Next to it was Sara's mother's grave. Olivia and Hetty stood on either side of Sara and Nanny Louisa was behind her as they slowly made their way towards the row of buggies. Reverend Leonard solemnly shook hands with everyone.

Sara had said nothing throughout the burial ceremony, but suddenly she stood stock-still in panic, and, grabbing her Nanny Louisa's hand, she held her back. She looked imploringly into the older woman's eyes.

"I had so many things I wanted to tell him. What am I going to do now? I'm frightened, Nanny."

Nanny Louisa put her arm around Sara, relieved that the child had finally spoken. "There is no need to be frightened, Sara," she said soothingly. "Remember, you're not alone."

At that moment, Sara felt more alone than she ever had in her entire life.

The empty black funeral cart pulled out of the graveyard, and in the distance, unnoticed by the mourners, six circus carts appeared against the horizon, their garish colors making a striking contrast against the leaden sky as they arrived in the village of Avonlea.

Chapter Nine

"And so, Miss Banks, the house in Montreal is under your trusteeship as well." The portly gentleman, with his spectacles riding low on his beak-like nose, handed Nanny Louisa a packet of money in a wallet. "I expect this will pay for any emergency expenses until you return to Montreal. Enclosed is Sara's allowance. She will receive the same amount each month."

Looking through the crack in the parlor door, Sara recognized the man as her father's lawyer, Mr. Bartholomew. He had been closeted with her two aunts and her Nanny Louisa for the past hour. She watched as Nanny Louisa accepted the money.

"Thank you, Mr. Bartholomew," she said quietly.

Mr. Bartholomew folded up his papers and took a deep breath. "I appreciate how difficult this must be for all of you, and I do apologize. However, the size and importance of the estate made it imperative that we have immediate discussions."

Hetty suddenly rose from the table and started to pace. Olivia made a small, pleading gesture to her to settle down, but Hetty was not to be silenced.

"I must say that I am deeply shocked that someone from outside the family would have been appointed Sara's guardian and trustee of her…considerable inheritance." Her voice shook with emotion.

Mr. Bartholomew looked up at her and raised his eyebrows, causing his glasses to fall even further down his nose.

"I can appreciate that, Miss King, but you must understand that Miss Banks has been with the Stanley family since—"

"Oh, I'm sure since time began," Hetty interrupted him. "But I would have thought that blood relations are of more import than longevity of employment." She picked up a sheaf of papers from the desk and shook it at the poor man. "This will is almost three years old! Had it been properly updated, as it should have been, why, quite clearly, Blair would have stipulated that Sara remain with us in Avonlea!"

"Well, that is not for me to say…" mumbled Mr. Bartholomew as he started to gather his papers together.

"But as Blair's lawyer, surely you should have advised him to keep it up to date." Hetty was not going to let him off easily.

"Miss King, Blair was still quite a young man. It was most unforeseen that such a tragic accident...that is to say, he probably gave very little practical thought to this—"

"Typical!" Hetty exploded bitterly. "Never thinking ahead, never thinking of the consequences—"

"Hetty" said Olivia warningly, but Hetty simply turned her back on them all.

In the hall, Sara bit her bottom lip. Her Nanny Louisa was on her feet now.

"I really must object, Mr. Bartholomew—"

Hetty turned back to her. "All I know is that Sara has not only lost her father, she has been severed from the family who love her."

Nanny Louisa squared her shoulders. "I assure you, my dear woman, that my love for Sara and my devotion to her are every bit the equal of yours."

"How dare you?" said Hetty, bristling.

Olivia could see that the two women were only going to make the situation worse if they continued along in this vein. She cleared her throat and gestured towards the door.

"May I see you for a moment, Hetty? In the kitchen?"

Something in Olivia's unusually urgent tone got through to Hetty. After excusing herself, she followed her younger sister towards the door.

Outside in the hall, Sara scurried up the stairs to avoid being caught listening, just as Olivia and Hetty appeared and went down the hall to the kitchen.

The minute the kitchen door swung closed behind them, Olivia turned to Hetty, her face beet-red with consternation.

"Hetty King! Where are your brains? Don't you ever learn anything? The tack you are taking didn't work with Blair and it won't work with Louisa Banks, either!"

Hetty was quite taken aback. "Tack! What tack?"

Olivia rolled her eyes in frustration. "You're putting everyone's back up! Now that will only ensure that Sara is taken away from us for good. Why can't you just bite your tongue for once?!"

Hetty was uncharacteristically silent for several seconds. How dare Olivia be so logical? It wasn't like her, not like her at all. Hetty didn't relish being talked to as her sister just had. On the other hand, she could see there was some sense to what Olivia had said, much as she hated to admit it.

"What do you suggest I do?" she hissed. "Bend over backwards to be nice to her?"

Olivia had that look on her face—the look she always wore when she knew she was right. "Yes. You can certainly catch more flies with honey than with vinegar."

Hetty hesitated. Olivia gave her a little push towards the door.

"Go on!"

Sara had crept down the stairs again and was listening to the low mumbles of her Nanny Louisa and Mr. Bartholomew when Hetty and Olivia walked through the kitchen door and came face to face with her.

"Sara Stanley!" said Hetty in surprise.

Sara, her face white, turned and dashed up the stairs. The sound of her footsteps was followed by a door slam. A worried frown formed on Hetty's face and she moved to follow her, but Olivia held her back. Just then, Louisa and Mr. Bartholomew emerged from the parlor.

"Ah, now, Miss King, Miss Banks and I have just been discussing Sara and when the most appropriate time would be to take her back to Montreal." Mr. Bartholomew had the look of a man who would rather be anywhere else in the world than where he found himself at that moment.

Hetty and Olivia looked shocked.

Nanny Louisa stepped forward, exasperated with the whole business.

"You needn't worry. I have no intention of taking Sara back yet. She is much too exhausted. We shall stay in Avonlea for at least a week, until I'm sure she is ready...if that's not too inconvenient for you, Miss King."

Hetty smiled, her new leaf turned firmly over.

"Inconvenient? Not at all! Please, stay as long as you wish. It would be an honor to have you as our guest, wouldn't it, Olivia?"

Olivia nodded quickly in approval, while Louisa J. Banks looked at both of them skeptically.

Mr. Bartholomew breathed a sigh of relief. "Fine, then, I must be on my way. I have a long trip back."

Louisa led him to the door, Hetty and Olivia following.

"Thank you again for coming all this way," Nanny Louisa said graciously. "Blair would have been so relieved to know things are being handled smoothly. You can see what I've been up against," she added, with a pointed look at her two hostesses.

Hetty glared at her, but Olivia gave her sister a look, and she immediately planted a smile on her face.

"Good day to you, Sir," she said to Mr. Bartholomew.

"The pleasure was mine." The lawyer gave the ladies a quick bow and then beat a hasty retreat.

Chapter Ten

Sara stood perfectly still, looking out her window, clutching her doll in her arms. How could the view from her room be the same? How could the breeze still ruffle her lace curtains and the sun throw such lovely dappled shadows on her rose-covered wallpaper? How long ago it seemed that she had stood looking out her window in Montreal. Waiting. Waiting for her father to come home. Again, that something stirred deep down within her, but she gritted her teeth, forbidding it to be become anything more than a mere flutter.

Her door opened behind her and she could feel her Aunt Hetty watching her.

"Eavesdroppers seldom hear good of themselves, or others..."

Sara didn't turn around, and Hetty realized that platitudes were perhaps not the sort of thing that were called for. How hard it was for her to tell Sara how she really felt. She had never been good at sharing her emotions. As a teacher, she had spent most of her life trying to cover them up. But the sight of the small, narrow back, stiff with grief and pride, touched her deeply.

"If I sounded a little...upset...about the way things have turned out, it is because...I feel this is where you truly belong."

Sara could feel tears rising, but she couldn't turn around and let her aunt see.

Hetty waited, desperate for Sara to help her through this difficult moment, but the back remained stiff and unmoving.

Hetty went on. "I understand how you must feel, but you have to...we all have to learn to face the cruelties in our lives." She groped for the words that would bring comfort to Sara. "You know, time will heal all." She went to touch Sara's shoulder. "We love you. You know that."

Sara couldn't respond. She felt a turmoil raging within her that she couldn't express. Hetty seemed about to say something more, but instead she gave Sara's shoulder a final squeeze and quietly left the room.

Sara continued to look out the window for a long time.

The golden glow of the lamps was the only cheerful sight in the Rose Cottage kitchen that night. Even though the sun had set hours ago, the heat was still oppressive, and Olivia, who was slowly stirring a pan of milk on the stove, wiped an errant strand of hair from her forehead. She and Hetty had decided the only way they were going to sleep that night was if they each had a cup of warm milk.

Olivia sighed. "I just wish she'd have a darn good cry. It seems so unnatural…I'm worried about her."

"She will deal with it in her own way, Olivia. The Kings are not ones to make a display of their grief…" Hetty glanced up as Nanny Louisa entered the room.

Without speaking to either of them, Louisa went to the hand-pump to fill the tea kettle. She jerked the handle up and down with no result and muttered under her breath. Finally, she attacked it more vigorously, only to get sprayed with water. She grabbed a dishcloth and wiped her dress off in disgust.

"Confounded pumps! Of all the archaic…"

Sara stood frozen for a second.
Then, springing into action, she ran to the fire bell
at the side of the store and pulled its rope frantically.
The bell clanged as more fireworks exploded.

❧❧❧❧

"Oh my Sara! My little Sara!
Is it really you? Glory! Glory!"
The gray hair blended with the gold
as they stood, embracing,
oblivious to Hetty King's glare.

❧❧❧

Blair Stanley grinned and caught his daughter,
swinging her around and around
until she was quite dizzy.

cx/cx/c

The woman grabbed the table.
Her eyes flew open and, as Sara watched, horrified,
they seemed to glow in their sockets
like two burning spheres.

"May we offer you some cocoa?" asked Olivia good-naturedly.

"No, thank you. But I'll take some up to Sara," said Louisa, straightening her shirtwaist and reclaiming her dignity.

"I already did," said Hetty, but Louisa ignored her and swept out of the room with the steaming cup.

Sara lay in her bed, staring at a photo of her father on the little table beside her. She heard footsteps coming up the stairs and quickly put the picture under her pillow. Nanny Louisa entered the room quietly and set the cup of cocoa beside Sara. A still-full cup of cocoa sat on the table.

"Drink this," she said, in the same stern tone she had used on Sara as she was growing up, and on Sara's father before her.

Sara watched her as she took Mr. Bartholomew's envelope of money out of her pocket and put it on top of the bureau. Nanny Louisa glanced at Sara's strained, white face and sat down on the bed. She stroked her forehead, in the way she always had since Sara was a baby.

"Sara, you should drink some of that," she said soothingly. "It would help you to sleep, child."

"I can't sleep," Sara replied bluntly. After a moment of silence, she gripped her nanny's hand. Louisa was surprised at how cold the child's hand was.

"Nanny Louisa...I hated all those people... talking about Papa...at the funeral. They didn't even know him. We're the only ones who really lost Papa. No one here can ever feel the way we do."

Louisa wiped her eyes. "I know, but your father would want life to go on. He would want us to be...brave."

There was another long moment of silence, broken only by the faint rattle of dishes as Olivia washed up in the kitchen. Sara stared at the ceiling of her room and the path of moonlight that cut across it from her window.

"I didn't even get to say goodbye to him."

Nanny Louisa's shoulders started to shake silently with sobs. Sara squeezed the older woman's hand and lay back in her bed.

Chapter Eleven

Peter Craig mopped his brow and continued chopping wood in front of the shed behind Rose Cottage. He couldn't fathom how anyone could stand cooking on a wood-stove in weather like this, but Miss King had demanded more wood, and who was he to say she was as crazy as a bedbug? He looked up and noticed Nanny Louisa as she crossed the lawn, heading to the outdoor privy.

Hetty watched her as well from the kitchen window, her eyes narrowed and her lips pursed with annoyance. A smell of burning sausages brought her back to earth with a bang and she rushed to turn them in the pan.

"Something burning?" Olivia asked innocently as she entered the kitchen.

"I don't know how many more mornings I will be able to listen to her go on about boiling the blasted water thoroughly before I make tea. As if there were a chance in creation that the water in Montreal could possibly be any purer than here."

Olivia hid a smile. "Now Hetty, you've been awfully good with her the last few days, I hope you won't ruin it all with a few hasty words. Where is she now, anyway?"

"She's in the privy out back. I hope she falls in," Hetty said vehemently as she tossed another piece of kindling into the wood-stove.

Suddenly there was a great banging and

yelling coming from the yard. The two women looked at each other and then stuck their heads out the door.

The banging was coming from the direction of the privy. It fairly rocked with the commotion. The little hook had fallen down into the eye on the outside of the door. Nanny Louisa had got herself locked in!

"Help me! Somebody let me out of here!" came her muffled cry as she pounded to get out.

Peter watched with great amusement as Hetty and Olivia came running from the house.

"How could anyone but a fool get themselves locked in an outhouse?" Hetty asked as she flicked the hook out of its catch.

Nanny Louisa was mortified as she came out, red-faced and indignant.

"A young girl of Sara's station ought not to be subjected to such primitive conditions if she is ever to come here again. And neither should I!"

"The outdoor privy has been good enough for three generations of Kings," said Hetty through clenched teeth. "I see no reason why we should replace it now."

Olivia glared at Hetty and looked pointedly at Louisa. Hetty immediately pasted a conciliatory smile on her face. "But of course, when I see it from your point of view, Louisa, yes, why...a child of Sara's present stature deserves better, certainly. Now please come in and have some breakfast. I've made those wheatcakes you enjoyed so much yesterday. And sausages."

Louisa J. Banks was not so easily fooled. "I couldn't eat a thing! I'm much too upset! And I'll tell you one thing, Hetty King, the facilities must be upgraded if Sara is ever to visit again, let alone live here! And I know that's what's on your mind. You can't fool me with your wheatcakes!"

The indignant lady stomped into the house, perfectly aware that Peter Craig was trying, without much success, to stifle his laughter.

As Nanny Louisa stormed through the kitchen, Hetty and Olivia following her, there was a knock on the front door. Before opening the house to visitors, Hetty carefully peeked out the front window to see who was there. The guests, she discovered, were Mrs. Potts and Reverend Leonard.

"Oh, good Lord!" she said under her breath, but it was too late. They'd seen her. Mrs. Potts gave her a little wave and she proceeded to the door.

Upstairs, Sara came out of her room dressed

in mourning black. Just as she reached the stairs, she could hear the drone of voices coming from the downstairs hall.

"I've brought you some of my stew, Hetty. I know it's not popular on hot summer nights but it's very fortifying. That Sara could use some meat on her bones."

"Olivia, get the Reverend a chair. Sit down Clara." Hetty's voice floated up the stairs to where Sara stood.

Sara tiptoed along the upstairs hall and started down the back stairs. Under no circumstance did she want to have to speak to either Reverend Leonard or Mrs. Potts. She looked into the kitchen to make sure it was empty and escaped out the back door.

Chapter Twelve

Peter Craig was just stacking the last piece of wood on the pile when he spotted Sara coming out the door. She looked around furtively and escaped around the corner of the house. Peter wiped his hands on his shirt and decided to catch up with her. Sara walked along the red-dirt road, her head down as Peter came up beside her.

"I haven't seen you since the funeral," he said, trying to start up a conversation. Sara was silent.

"I'm sorry about your father," he tried again. It really hurt to see Sara so obviously miserable. "I liked him," he said simply, and Sara turned and acknowledged him for the first time.

"Sara, are you all right?" Peter asked.

Sara glanced away. "Yes, thank you."

Peter was uncomfortable. Sara was just not like her old self. "Sara, I wish I could do something," he mumbled.

"It's all right, Peter," said Sara, as they fell into step with each other.

Suddenly, from over the top of the hill, Peter could see the tops of tents in the distance. "Do you want to go to the circus with me?" he burst out. "I've saved some money. I'll treat."

"No, thank you," said Sara.

"Aw, c'mon Sara!" Peter coaxed. "Felix says there's a fellow there who swallows fire. Maybe it'll cheer you up."

Sara looked at Peter and smiled wanly. She hesitated for a moment and then decided.

"Maybe I will!"

For a second, Peter could see the old Sara Stanley, the one who could never turn down the possibility of an adventure. He grinned and ran across the field towards the tents, and Sara followed him.

The raucous music of calliopes and hurdy-gurdies competed with the slang of carnival barkers and the call of the ringmaster. A lady with a parasol walked slowly across a tightrope strung against a background of circus banners, the bangles on her arms flashing in the sunlight as she balanced herself. Sara and Peter tried to keep their eyes on everything at once, completely captivated by the sights and smells that surrounded them.

A small group of gaudily painted circus caravans surrounded a main tent and two or three smaller, striped tents. The ringmaster posed theatrically in front of the main circus tent and tried his best to draw in the crowds.

"Ladies and gentlemen of Avonlea!" he shouted. "Come one, come all to the Bunburry Brothers traveling road show!"

Peter crept behind the man and lifted the side of the tent flap to get a look at what might be inside. Sara was about to follow him when a clown spotted Peter and instantly grabbed him by the scruff of the neck.

"Come on! Get out! Scalawags!"

Sara stared at the man in fright. The clown face was anything but happy. In fact, only half of it was completed, as if they had interrupted him in the middle of applying his make-up. Peter shook him off and took Sara's hand, dragging her to a different area.

"Step inside and see it all!" the ringmaster called. "We have jugglers, acrobats, fire-eaters, snake-charmers and Barney the Dancing Bear!"

As Peter and Sara rounded a corner, they came face to face with Barney the Dancing Bear.

"Wow!" breathed Peter as he moved closer.

The bear's owner pushed him away roughly. "Don't touch the bear," he growled. "He'll bite your head off!"

"Friendly people," said Peter, as he and Sara walked away.

Strange, grotesque faces watched the two children as they made their way between the tents. Peter seemed oblivious to them, but Sara was beginning to feel a little frightened. A juggler caught Peter's attention as he deftly handled five very sharp-looking swords, sending them dancing and flashing through the air and catching them all in turn.

Sara was wondering if she shouldn't just go home when she spotted a circus cart with a painted sign on its side and a striped blue tent behind it. Slowly, Sara walked towards it. The sign read "Isis, Spiritualist. Reunite with your loved ones. Talk with your dearly departed."

Intrigued, Sara drew closer to it, almost in a daze. Somewhere in the distance she could hear the ringmaster still bellowing to the crowd.

"Don't miss Isis! Have your fortunes told, futures revealed. Get your tickets and step right up!"

Suddenly, Peter was beside her, tugging at her sleeve. "Sara! Come and see the snake!"

Sara didn't answer, and Peter, too excited to wait, rushed off. When the snake-charmer withdrew tantalizingly into his tent, offering greater wonders, but only for paying customers, Peter again looked for Sara. He saw her heading resolutely for the fortune-teller's tent, and he ran over to her and grabbed her arm just as she was about to go through the beaded curtain that served as its doorway.

"You don't wanna go in there, Sara," said Peter. His mother had told him all about fortune-tellers and fakers. They weren't to be trusted.

But Sara turned to him with an almost feverish glow in her eyes. "Please, Peter, come with me! I have to know what it's all about!"

She pulled Peter towards the beaded curtain, and, just as they reached it, a swarthy-looking Gypsy woman appeared. She slowly pushed the beads aside. Her face was sharp and bird-like, the eyes heavily made-up and outlined in black. She was dressed in a blue-and-gold Egyptian costume. Her bright eyes took Sara in with a glance.

"Come in, child. I've been expecting you," she said, her voice so low that it was almost inaudible.

Peter jumped in surprise and Sara drew in her breath. She stared into the woman's eyes and, dividing the ropes of beads, entered the tent. As she passed through, Peter tried to follow her, but the woman's arm blocked his way.

"Only one at a time, boy," she said, and disappeared into the darkness of the tent.

The beads clacked and tinkled behind her as they fell back into place.

Chapter Thirteen

Sara entered the tent slowly. She could feel the eyes of the Gypsy woman on her back. Suddenly, the woman was in front of her, gazing at her intently. She led Sara to a small table and, pulling out a chair, indicated that she should sit. Sara sat, and the woman sank gracefully into a chair across from her.

"I am Isis," she said, in the same low, gravelly voice, her eyes never once leaving Sara's face. "Please sit down...Sara."

Sara's eyes widened. "How did you know my name?"

The woman took Sara's palm and held it in a firm grip. A slight smile curved her heavily rouged lips.

"Isis knows all."

Sara swallowed. The woman, Isis, finally turned her gaze from Sara to the little crystal ball that stood in the middle of the table.

"You are not from around here," she said. "I see a large city..."

"Yes," said Sara, hardly daring to breath. "I'm from Montreal..."

Isis continued to stare into the depths of the crystal. "Such a great sadness you carry with you. There is someone who is trying to contact you. Someone who was very close to you."

Sara gripped the edge of the table. She felt as if she were going to faint.

"It is your father, isn't it?" Isis jerked her

head up and looked sharply at Sara's white face.

Sara nodded slowly, unable to speak.

Isis looked at her with piercing eyes. Eyes like a parrot, thought Sara. Like a parrot in the zoo...in Montreal, when Papa and I used to...

"When the spirit moves me," Isis resumed, "I have successfully been able to communicate with the beyond. But," she said slyly, "of course, anything of worth carries a price..."

Sara reached into her pocket and put a coin on the table. "I have money."

Isis picked up the coin and turned it around in her fingers with obvious disappointment. "I will do my best."

She stared once again into her crystal ball. A flame appeared from a candle on the table, though no visible hand had lit it. The tent became very dark, as though the sunlight filtering through the sides of the tent had been dismissed. Isis closed her eyes and started to sway gently.

"Your father's name was...Blair..."

"Yes—Blair Stanley," stammered Sara, her lips dry, her heart beating rapidly.

Isis moaned, and her body began waving back and forth more violently.

"Blair Stanley...can you hear me? Blair Stanley?"

Her voice rose. The candle flickered; its light threw shadows on the cheesecloth behind where she sat. The woman grabbed the table. Her eyes flew open and, as Sara watched, horrified, they seemed to glow in their sockets like two burning spheres. Shadows danced on the curtain behind her head. Her face began to shine with an eerie green light. She raised her arms to the ceiling, momentarily hiding her face, and small explosions of smoke and flashes of light emanated from around her. Suddenly, she flung her arms away from her face, and where human eyes should have been, there were white orbs without pupils, as if her eyes had turned backwards into her head.

Sara was stiff with terror. The shadows continued to dance around the walls. The table seemed to float. Isis was in a trance! The red gash of her rouged lips opened and she began to speak in a low monotone.

"He is looking for his little daughter. He needs to say goodbye."

Two loud thumps made Sara jump, and she became aware of the shadowy image of a man forming very slowly and indistinctly behind

Isis's head. Sara felt that she couldn't move if she wanted to.

"He wants you to know that he misses you, but that he is very peaceful."

The image of a tall man became slightly sharper. Sara could hardly breathe. A scream caught in her throat and threatened to choke her. The man looked like her father!

The monotonous voice continued.

"He is with your mother. I feel there is something they must tell you...oh, yes, it is of utmost importance. He is trying so hard to speak..."

"Papa! It's me!" Sara burst out.

"It is very difficult to understand." Isis was moaning now, weaving back and forth as if in agony. Her voice grew higher and higher and she raised her arms above her head, clutching at the air, her arms' shadows looking like dancing snakes on the cloth behind her. The image of the man became fainter and fainter.

"Papa! Don't go!" Sara cried. "I'm here, Papa. It's me! Come back! Can't you hear me, Papa?" She started to sob.

The curtain behind Isis went blank, and when she suddenly opened her eyes, they were as clear and as piercing as before.

"There is no more I can do. His spirit is very,

very difficult to reach. He has gone too far away now."

"Oh, please try! I must speak to him! Please!" begged Sara, as she leapt up from her chair, grasping the table.

Isis shook her head. "I don't know if he will ever come back," she said dismissively.

"Please. You've got to try again."

"Perhaps later," the woman said wearily. Then she looked up at Sara, her eyes slits. "But of course, it will cost more...much, much more."

"I have lots of money at home!" Sara blurted out.

Isis gripped Sara's wrist with surprising strength.

"Very well. Speak not of this to anyone. It makes my bridge to the spirits weak. Your father is distant as it is. Come back...alone. Tell no one, do you understand?"

Sara nodded mutely.

A bright green-and-red parrot was happily standing on Peter's head when he spotted Sara, walking between the tents.

"Sara, come and meet Captain Bligh!" he shouted to her.

"Captain Bligh! Captain Bligh!" croaked the

parrot, and with a squawk it flew back to its owner, who sat smoking on the steps of a run-down cart.

"Sara!" Peter called again.

Sara didn't answer. She walked along, totally immersed in her own thoughts. Peter ran after her and caught up.

"Sara! Did you see? That man put that parrot on my head. It can talk! And guess what else I saw! There's a fella back there who can stand on his head with no hands."

Sara continued to walk, not saying a word. Peter looked at her curiously.

"What's the matter?"

"Nothing, " replied Sara softly, and then she looked at him sideways. "Can you keep a secret?"

"I guess so," Peter said, expectantly.

Sara fixed her blue eyes on Peter. "The fortune-teller...she contacted my father...she spoke to him."

Her face was white and drawn, obviously serious about what she had just said. Peter looked at her with disbelief, and before he could stop himself he burst out laughing.

"You don't believe that hogwash, do you?"

A flush started up Sara's cheeks. "Peter, I saw him!"

Peter smiled at her, still chuckling.

Sara turned on her heel and strutted down the path towards the circus exit.

"Fine! Then don't believe me! I don't care!"

She started to run. Peter frowned. She was serious. She really was. He started running after her.

"Sara! Come back! I believe you…!"

Inside the tent, Isis blew out the candle on her table and rose from her chair, her face a mask. She took off one of her gold hoop earrings.

"Leo!" she bellowed, her accent course and vulgar and totally unlike the voice of the mysterious Isis.

A tall man, heavy and muscular, appeared from the folds of the tent.

"I told you she'd come," Isis said smugly without looking up at him. "No kid can resist a circus, no matter what." She removed her other earring and tossed it on the table.

"But you let her get away," the man said.

"She'll be back. She bought it." Her voice was so low that it was almost lost in the noise of the circus beyond their tent.

"We play this right and it could be our ticket out of this stinkin' circus," growled the man.

Isis looked at him sharply, her parrot eyes glaring at him.

"Don't you remember why we're stuck in this stinking circus? Because you got carried away in the last town, taking that old lady's life savings so she could talk to her bloody dead cat! Too bad her son was the town judge, wasn't it? You let *me* handle this!"

"Shut up!" snarled Leo. But then a small smile formed on his face. He chuckled and unfolded a dirty old Charlottetown newspaper to a picture of Sara and an article about a Mr. Blair Stanley's unfortunate death.

"An heiress. A genuine heiress."

Chapter Fourteen

Sara gazed at herself in the mirror above her small dressing table. She was wearing her new blue dress covered with lace, the one her father had given her. It seemed so long ago now. She straightened the ribbon around its waist and, closing her eyes for just a moment, took a deep breath. So far she had been very lucky. Hetty and Olivia were outside hanging laundry and Nanny Louisa was having a nap. She didn't relish coming face to face with any of them. She turned from the mirror and crossed her room to the tall mahogany dresser, where Nanny Louisa's wallet still lay where she had left it. Sara hesitated as she reached for it. She wasn't really stealing, she told herself. It was her money. Mr. Bartholomew had said so. She decisively picked up the wallet and headed towards her door. She paused only a moment as she caught a glimpse of her father's photograph on her bedside table, and then she was gone.

As Sara disappeared down the red, dusty road towards Avonlea, Hetty and Olivia were busy hanging the wash in the back garden. Louisa J. Banks, fresh from her nap, emerged from the house and headed towards them at a brisk pace.

"Where is Sara?" she demanded in her crisp, governess voice. "She's been gone for hours. I suppose she has been allowed to run completely wild," she added, watching the white sheets catch the wind and billow out against the blue sky.

"Not at all, Louisa," Olivia mumbled. She took the wooden clothespins out of her mouth. "Sara has learned to be very responsible since she came to Avonlea. "

Hetty shook her head. "Goodness knows I

didn't want to talk to Clara Potts either. She's a bore at the best of times. Sara's probably visiting Felicity."

"I hope so," said Olivia, her brow furrowing with concern. "It would do her good."

Nanny Louisa was not to be convinced. "Well, if Sara had disappeared for hours at a time when she was at home, there'd be only one explanation...trouble!"

Hetty rolled her eyes and viciously stabbed at a dishcloth with a clothespin. "That may be true in a dreadful city like Montreal, but there is very little trouble a child can get into in Avonlea. Everyone has an eye out for everyone else."

If only Hetty knew.

The tent was empty. Dust floated in the air, illuminated by the sunlight as it filtered through the striped canvas. The flap moved and Sara peeked in. She entered quietly, holding tightly to the wallet, and looked around. In the brighter light it no longer seemed as mysterious. She wondered how Isis had made it so dark before. Then she spotted some black canvas rolled up at the top of the tent, held with ropes. If they were untied, she could see that the canvas would drop down like a blind, cutting off the light. But who could have untied them? Isis had been alone with her in the tent.

Her thoughts were interrupted by a slight rustling sound coming from the cheesecloth that rose behind the little table. Suddenly, a shadow began to form. A shadow of a man…in the same place she had seen the image of her father!

"Papa!" Sara whispered. Then there was a small explosion, accompanied by a flash of blue-green light and a puff of smoke. Sara's heart began to thump painfully in her chest, but the illusion was quickly shattered.

"Bloody thing!" came a very human male voice.

Sara jumped as another shadow joined the first one.

"Now what are ya doing?"

The female voice was very familiar. Sara hid herself behind one of the folds of the canvas and watched silently.

"Workin' on your ghosts! What do ya think?" came the gruff voice of the man.

"Well, don't get too fancy. That kid's smart. She might get suspicious of too much hocus-pocus."

A man emerged from behind the cheese-cloth, rubbing his hand as if he had hurt it. He was carrying an armful of small, round containers. One of them toppled off the top of his pile and landed with another small explosion. Puffs of colored smoke rose from it. The empty tin rolled directly towards where Sara was hiding. She could see the skull-and-crossbones sign and read its label easily: "Danger. Concussion Powder. Explodes on impact!"

Suddenly, a woman appeared from behind the same curtain.

"Isis!" thought Sara.

"Don't throw that stuff around," Isis spat at the man, and she walked swiftly over to the tin, bending down to pick it up. As she did so, she spotted a pretty blue satin shoe under the folds of the tent. Her eyes narrowed, and with amazing speed she ripped back the canvas to reveal Sara, her eyes wide with fear.

"You're early, Sara Stanley," she whispered.

A fury of anguish rose up in Sara.

"I trusted you! You stole from me! I'm going to tell the constable!"

Sara turned and bolted towards the flap of the tent, but Leo grabbed her from behind. Sara struggled and kicked but to no avail; the man was too strong. A large hand covered her mouth as she tried to scream and call out.

"Leo! What are you doing? This is going too far!" Isis hissed at her accomplice as she tried to pull his arms away from Sara. Sara struggled, but he put one arm around her throat and the other over her nose and mouth. Her head began to ache and the room started to spin.

"Are you crazy?" he growled. "You heard her! She was going to the police!"

Sara fought against a rising darkness. Leo started to drag her towards the back of the tent, his grip tightening. Isis followed, still trying to talk some sense into the man.

"Forget about it, Leo! This is kidnapping!"

Sara was beginning to lose consciousness. Through a fog of light and dark, she could hear the man's voice, as if in a dream.

"Shut up! This is my big chance! The kid's worth a fortune."

Chapter Fifteen

Nanny Louisa paced the parlor in Rose Cottage.

"I knew something was amiss. Sara would never just go off like this! If anything's happened to her..." She left the sentence unfinished.

"Don't upset yourself so, Louisa," said Olivia, trying to remain calm herself, but not quite succeeding. "Alec is out looking for her."

Louisa sighed and walked towards the front hall, and Hetty continued to peer through the front window.

Ever since it had been discovered that Sara was in fact not at the King Farm and not playing with Felicity, Rose Cottage had been in a state of alarm. No one could remember exactly when she had left the house. Hetty believed it was while that infernal Clara Potts had been visiting, but Olivia reminded them that Sara had not even appeared for breakfast.

"Too much confusion," Hetty thought to herself bitterly.

Peter Craig was in the kitchen doing some of his own pacing. He was caught in a dilemma. He had promised to keep a secret and he felt bound to honor that vow, but surely this was an exception. He hated to see everyone so upset. When he heard the sound of buggy wheels, he crossed his fingers. This was probably Alec King returning, and most likely Sara was with him. He wouldn't have to tell after all.

It was Alec King, but no Sara sat next to him in the buggy. All three women rushed to meet him at the door and hear his news.

"I asked everywhere," he said flatly, running

his hand through his hair. "No one has seen hide nor hair of Sara."

"Oh, good Lord!" said Nanny Louisa, as she sank back against the banister.

"Where could she be?" Olivia's voice sounded dangerously close to tears.

Behind the kitchen door, Peter straightened his shoulders and made a decision. He pushed the door open and entered the hallway. All four grown-ups turned and looked at him.

"I think I know where she might be..." he said in a small voice, the toe of his boot digging into the carpet.

"What are you talking about, Peter?" Hetty swooped down on him like a hawk.

"Where?" demanded Alec.

"At the circus," Peter replied, facing them.

If he had said Sara was in Timbuktu, Hetty could not have looked more flabbergasted. "The circus!"

Peter pushed on. "I told Sara she shouldn't talk to that old fake!"

"Fake! What fake?" Hetty sputtered.

"The fortune-teller. Sara said she...could talk to her father."

The grown-ups looked at him with their

mouths open. Alec lost no time. He was out the door and pulling away in the buggy before anyone could say another word.

In a thick grove of maple trees off the main road leading away from Avonlea, Isis and Leo were very busy. The sign that read "Isis, Spiritualist. Reunite with your loved ones. Talk with your dearly departed" had been removed from the side of their cart and they were in the process of stowing it away underneath the belly of the vehicle. Now it no longer resembled a Gypsy caravan. It could have belonged to any number of nomadic travelers making their way across the Island, and it was sure not to attract any undo attention.

Isis worked alongside her cohort, but she was far from calm.

"The kid's been out cold for hours, Leo. Are you sure you didn't kill her with that chloroform?" she asked, her eyes darting, looking for anyone who might have strayed off the road.

Leo's shoulders started to shake with mirth. "The princess is just gettin' her beauty sleep, that's all." He was delighted by his own pathetic attempt at humor.

Inside the cart, the sound of his laughter

penetrated the darkness of Sara's dreams. She opened her eyes and was overcome by a wave of dizziness. Gradually, her eyes became focused and she slowly looked around at her surroundings. Memory of her struggle in the tent came flooding back, and instantly she was gripped with fear. She tried to scream, but her throat was dry and parched and nothing would come out.

Suddenly the cart lurched and started to roll forward. Sara desperately wanted to look through a little round window that was directly above her, but her body would not obey the signals that her brain was sending to it. She tried to clear her mind, to think what the best course of action would be. Above all, she knew she mustn't let her terror immobilize her.

The cart was definitely moving, along a very bumpy back road by the feel of it. Then, after another lurch and bump, the way was smoother. They must be on a main road, Sara thought to herself. She was much less dizzy now, and her eyes focused. Costumes lined the walls of the cart. On the floor was an old carpet, stained and worn. Sara stared. Where the carpet had been pushed aside, there was a hole in the floor. She could see the road moving past her underneath. She was hit with a brilliant idea. She instantly kicked her shoe off and let it fall through the hole in the floor down to the road below. Then she started ripping small pieces of lace from her dress and let them float downwards through the hole as well. She hoped that someone would find them, that they would serve as a path for someone to follow.

Suddenly the cart pulled off onto a bumpy stretch of road again, and Sara was thrown off balance. She toppled roughly and painfully against the edge of a small bunk attached to the side of the cart. Grabbing onto its sides for support, she peered through the dirty window at the branches of trees as they scraped and scratched against it. The cart came to a sudden halt. Sara lay down on the bunk and waited. A wave of dizziness passed over her. A horse whinnied, and then came the sound of heavy boots. The back doors of the cart flew open. Sara shut her eyes and faked unconsciousness.

The woman was the first to speak.

"We've gone far enough, Leo. If we're caught with this child we'll be arrested. We have to let her go..."

"Shut up, Isis!" Leo cut her off. "I'm runnin' this show now. If you don't like it, get out!" His eyes started to shine. "Think what she's worth to her kin! A king's ransom!"

He went over to Sara and grabbed her by the shoulder. Sara cried out in spite of herself.

"So," he bellowed, "you're awake! Good!" He bent down so low and close to her face that Sara thought she would faint from the heat of his breath. "Her Highness just has to tell us where she lives and sign a little ransom note I've written just for her!"

Sara stared at Isis and Leo. The woman's face was expressionless as Leo broke into another bout of hearty laughter.

Chapter Sixteen

The sun was sinking low in the sky as Alec King reached the circus grounds. Most of the crowd had dispersed, leaving the small gathering of tents looking almost deserted. Alec jumped down from the buggy and approached a group of circus performers who were lounging near the main entrance. With their make-up smeared or half removed, they looked warily at Alec, their faces stony and closed.

"Do you have a fortune-telling act traveling with you?" Alec asked them.

The performers looked at each other, entering into a silent pact, and then the tallest of the bunch looked Alec right in the eye. "No," he said sullenly. "Nobody around here like that!" He shifted his gaze to the others, who shook their heads.

Not yet discouraged, Alec spotted another group gathered around the ringmaster, who was counting the day's proceeds. Alec walked towards them. They ignored him at first, but he cleared his throat and they looked up laconically.

"Maybe you fellas can help me," Alec began. "I'm looking for a little blond girl with blue eyes."

The motley group continued to watch him with veiled eyes.

"She was here with the fortune-teller."

A man in a tattered clown costume spat tobacco on the ground. No one else said or did anything.

"You had a fortune-teller act here, traveling with you? Isn't that right?" Alec insisted, feeling his temper beginning to rise.

"I didn't see anyone," said the ringleader slowly. "Sorry."

Alec could see that he was going to learn nothing from these people. He turned on his heel in frustration and walked away.

"Something's not right here," he mumbled to himself. He climbed into the buggy and headed for Avonlea. He needed help and he needed it fast.

"Everything's under control, Alec. I've got men looking everywhere." Alec paced back and forth in the parlor of Rose Cottage. Abner Jeffries was trying to calm him down. The sun had set long ago and still there was no sign of Sara. Nanny Louisa sat silently in a chair in the shadows of the room, Olivia next to her holding her hand.

"You couldn't find a lost cow, let alone a child, Abner," Hetty uttered from where she stood at the window, her back straight as a ramrod.

Nanny Louisa stirred in her chair. "Rather than taking the law into your own hands, as seems to be your habit, hadn't you better contact the Charlottetown police?"

Abner turned and addressed her as courteously as he could. "I assure you, Ma'am, that those steps have been taken. But they advised me that, in a case like this, it's sometimes better to sit tight."

"Sit tight?!" Alec exploded.

"Well, Alec, Sara has been known to fly the coop before, you know. Have you checked your own barn?"

Alec looked at Abner as though he could cheerfully wring his neck. "You must think this is some kind of joke, Abner," he said quietly. "I have searched every inch of this farm. Felix and Andrew have combed the woods. Felicity and Janet have checked with all the neighbors. She is lost, man, or...kidnapped, and we have to do everything in our power to find her." The more Alec thought about it, the more convinced he became that Sara's disappearance was connected with the mysterious fortune teller.

"I wish you'd calm down, Alec! We're all doin' our best!" said Abner.

Alec picked up his coat. "I know, I know..."

"Now where are you goin'?" Abner asked as Alec headed for the door.

"If you want to 'sit tight,' you can," said Alec. "But I can't sit around anymore! I'm going out to look for her again."

Alec stalked out of the house. The door slammed and his horse could soon be heard galloping away.

Abner shuffled into the hall, twisting and turning his hat in his hands. "I'll be on my way, too." He turned back to the women as he reached the door. "We'll do our best, Hetty. As I say, I've got men scouring the countryside. I'll go join them."

Chapter Seventeen

Sara laid the pen down on the overturned crate that had served as a desk. Leo's hand swept down and picked up the piece of paper that Sara had just put her signature on. He looked at it triumphantly and read it.

"If you want to see the child alive, leave ten thousand dollars at the Avonlea covered bridge tomorrow at midnight." Once again, he shook with laughter. "We'll be rich, Isis! Leo's the smart one, isn't he?!"

Isis grabbed the note out of his hands with a sneer. "Oh yes! So smart! Now let me deliver this."

Leo grabbed it back from her. "No, you might be recognized."

Before Isis could protest, he stomped out of the cart and slammed the doors. The sound of a padlock snapping shut followed. Isis sat down quietly and sullenly, avoiding Sara's gaze. Sara stared at her, her eyes brimming with tears.

"I believed you," she said quietly. She turned to the wall and her body started to heave with sobs.

"No, you believed what you wanted to believe, like all the rest," Isis replied sadly, almost to herself.

Sara continued to weep. The woman looked at her, and with something approaching pity, she got up and covered the crying child with a blanket.

A shadow crossed the back garden of Rose Cottage, snaking its way furtively between the trees and bushes behind the house. It stopped suddenly, like an animal, listening for sounds from within the house. Sensing that no one was around, the figure crossed to the back door and stuffed a letter under it. Then it ran towards the shrubs.

Peter Craig came out of the woodshed just in time to see the shape of a man disappear through the hedge. He dropped the wood he was carrying and ran towards the hedge in pursuit.

"Hey, you! Come back!" he cried. "Miss King! Help!"

Leo looked around and saw the boy running across the lawn. He turned and thrashed his way through the bushes and disappeared into the darkness of the surrounding woods.

Peter ran after him, the branches scratching his face, the undergrowth tripping him up. He stopped, panting for breath. The figure had disappeared.

Hetty was the first to run into the kitchen from the parlor, with Nanny Louisa and Olivia close behind her. She spotted the note on the floor almost immediately and grabbed it with trembling hands.

Isis dozed, her head resting on the crate. Sara lay on the filthy bunk, staring at the ceiling and watching the morning rays of the sun just begin to shed light on the interior of the cart. Suddenly there was the sound of a lock being opened. The cart doors were flung open and Leo entered. Sara pretended to be asleep.

"Wake up!" Leo hissed at Isis, shaking her shoulder until she awoke. "Why isn't she tied up?" he asked angrily, pointing at Sara.

"She can't go far, can she?" said Isis, yawning and rubbing her eyes.

Sara sat bolt upright in the bunk, startling both of them. "When they find me, they'll put you in jail for the rest of your lives!" she spat at them.

Furious, Leo grabbed a rope hanging from the wall of the cart and attempted to tie Sara's hands. She struggled and succeeded in biting him hard on the back of his hand. He yowled in pain.

"You're hurting her!" yelled Isis, grabbing at him. "Stop it, Leo!"

"*I'm* hurting *her*?" he cried, still rubbing his hand. "She's a wildcat!"

Isis pushed him with amazing strength, sending him backwards against the doors of the cart. Sara cringed against the wall, terrified.

Alec's shoulders were slumped with weariness as he traveled on horseback along one of the side roads that eventually led to Markdale. Throughout the night, he had covered all but three of the possible routes out of Avonlea. Now, as the sun was just beginning to show itself along the horizon and the dew glistened on the grass and the daisies that lined the sides of the road, he saw something unusual on the ground in front of him, and his pulse quickened.

"Whoa!" he said, as he reined in the horse. He swung his leg over and dropped to the ground.

There were fresh buggy tracks apparent, but something else far more interesting lay on the road. He stooped down and picked up a blue satin shoe. It was unmistakably Sara's. He looked at the tracks on the road, ran back to his horse and mounted up.

He spurred the horse on but stopped again suddenly, spying the bits of lace that floated along the road in the morning breeze. His heart pounding, he followed the ruts of cart wheels until they disappeared from the soil of the main road. To his left was an overgrown cow path. The cart must have turned in there.

Sara hid her face as Leo picked himself up and rubbed his bruised shoulder. Isis looked at him defiantly, but the look disappeared as he walked towards her with threatening eyes.

"You'll do as I say!" he warned. "Tie her up!"

Isis backed away. "I don't want any part of this anymore!"

He continued towards her. "Fine, then you won't get one penny of the money!"

"And what if they don't pay the ransom, Leo? What then?" she asked sarcastically.

"They'll pay if they ever want to see her pretty face again," he said quietly, and Sara could tell that he meant it.

"What's that supposed to mean?" asked Isis, her voice flat.

"Why don't you shut up and quit askin' questions," snarled Leo.

"I told you, Leo, I won't let you hurt her!" said Isis, but Sara realized the woman was beginning to be as terrified as she was.

Alec led his horse down the path and suddenly, as he rounded a bend, he discovered the cart, pulled up behind a grove of trees. He approached it silently and quickly, using the dense growth of the bush as cover. As he got closer, he could hear voices raised in argument.

"I don't want to be any part of this, you idiot!" a woman's voice cried out shrilly. "I've had enough. Do you hear me?"

Then he could have sworn he heard the sound of a child crying. Sara! He stepped forward too quickly in his haste to get to her and a twig snapped loudly under his foot.

Inside the cart, Leo stood stock-still and listened. He crouched by the window and looked out. Sara strained to follow his gaze. The man narrowed his eyes as he watched Alec approach. Sara saw him too. She started to scream and call for him.

"Uncle Al—"

Leo clamped his hand roughly over her

mouth. "Keep her quiet," he hissed at Isis, "or you'll both answer to me!"

He picked up his gun and crept towards the doors of the cart. Sara kicked and thrashed around as Isis tried to cover her mouth with a scarf. One of her kicking motions knocked the woman's arm away, and in that moment of freedom Sara screamed again as loud as she could.

Alec heard Sara's scream and continued to run to the cart, heading towards the double doors at the back. Suddenly he came face to face with Leo, who appeared around the corner of the cart, his gun pointed straight at Alec.

"You take another step, I'll shoot," said the man, his face twitching nervously.

Alec froze.

"Uncle Alec!" came the pitiful sound of Sara's voice from the cart. "He's got a gun!"

Alec moved deliberately towards the cart, his eyes daring the man to shoot.

Leo started to sweat, but his shaking finger pulled the trigger as Alec made a final run. The sound of the gunfire echoed and reverberated through the silence of the clearing, and Alec fell to the ground.

Chapter Eighteen

Leo paced back and forth, while Isis watched him with narrowed, sullen eyes. Things were not going according to plan. Side by side on the bunk, Alec and Sara were tied up, their hands and feet bound tightly. A red stain spread on the shoulder of Alec's white shirt where the bullet had grazed him.

"Please, let the girl go." Alec appealed to them once again, wearily. "Believe me, I'll gladly stay and help you get off the Island."

"Both of you are goin' nowhere until the ransom is paid tonight," said Leo bluntly, and he stomped out of the cart.

Alec sighed, and, in obvious pain, he tried to shift around to see where the man had gone. Isis watched, her face an impassive mask.

"You need a doctor," Sara said, looking up at her uncle, her eyes wide with sympathy and worry.

"Don't worry about that. It's nothing. It's just a graze," said Alec.

Sara bit her lip. A wave of remorse swept through her.

"Oh, Uncle Alec! I'm so sorry I got you into all of this trouble. Please don't hate me."

"What?" said Alec, looking down at the bowed head beside him. "I don't hate you, Sara."

"But you were so angry with me..." The words came out slowly. "Over the fireworks..."

"Well, of course I was angry! I get cross at Felix half a dozen times a day when he gets out of line. It's because I love him."

Sara struggled with her emotions. Something was stirring way down deep, something she had buried a long time ago.

Alec's voice continued, softly. "And I...love you too, Sara...like my own daughter. If I didn't, I probably wouldn't care enough to get angry."

"Papa says that too." The words came unbidden. The minute she said them, something burst in Sara. The dreadful, dark, empty, helpless feeling she had been hiding for weeks, ever since her father had died, threatened to rush to the surface and overwhelm her. She fought it.

"Sara...why did you even talk to these people?" Alec asked gently.

"I just wanted to see if..." It was so difficult to explain. How could she begin? "I just wanted to see him, once more. Oh, Uncle Alec, he can't be gone…really gone…" Sara started to cry. "I just can't…realize it!"

Alec leaned against her, hoping that his mere presence would take some of the hurt away.

"It's all right Sara…it takes a long time to…to realize it…"

"But I miss him so much. I just wanted to see him…" The tears flowed down her face and her shoulders shook.

Alec rocked against her, cursing the ropes that held his hands and arms. "I know…I know…I understand…" he said quietly.

"And the worst thing is…" Sara sobbed, the ache in her soul reaching a peak, "I never got to say goodbye. I didn't say goodbye…"

The floodgates burst, and Sara sobbed uncontrollably against Alec's shoulder.

"That's my girl…" he said soothingly. "There now…cry all you want. Sara, I know it's hard to accept this now, but your father will never be lost to you, as long as you have him in your heart."

Sara still sobbed, but she felt a great weight lifting from her heart. The sadness would always be there, but, as she leaned against her uncle, she had taken her first step towards accepting her loss.

They had both totally forgotten Isis, who sat as still as a statue watching them, visibly moved. She rose quietly and went out the doors.

She rounded the corner of the cart and came upon Leo, asleep with his gun and hat on the ground next to him. Isis looked at him and then set off quietly into the bush.

Janet King sat at the kitchen table in Rose Cottage crying and dabbing at her eyes, Felicity by her side. Nanny Louisa brought Janet a cup of tea and patted her on the shoulder. Over the last few hours she had found herself becoming closer to this group of people, people who, in the past, she had always assiduously avoided.

"Why did he have to be so bullheaded and go off on his own?" sobbed Janet.

Louisa gave her another reassuring pat. "Now don't you worry. Everyone is doing all they can. Alec is sure to be just fine."

"I should have talked to Sara," said Felicity, in a small voice. "I just didn't know what to say. I can't imagine how I would feel if my father died."

At the mere mention of the possibility, Janet let out a howl and buried her face in her hankie.

Hetty and Louisa exchanged understanding glances.

"We're all full of those thoughts, child," said Hetty briskly. "But hindsight is no substitute for foresight. Now pull yourself together, Janet."

Hetty felt the need to do something, anything. She was never very good at standing around waiting for other people to do things for her, and she had found the last few hours intolerable. She had no idea what to do about the ransom note. They had not even mentioned it to Janet—the woman couldn't cope as it was. Ten thousand dollars, my auntie! she thought. What kind of numbskull would think they could get their hands on that kind of money by midnight! She left the little group and went out onto the porch, glad of the fresh air.

Chapter Nineteen

In the cart, Sara had stopped sobbing and now leaned weakly against Alec.

"Now, you and I are going to get out of this," said Alec, with more strength of spirit than he actually felt. Hampered by the tight ropes, he reached awkwardly for Sara's hand and touched it to the side of the bunk. "Feel that sharp edge? Just rub the rope against it."

Sara started to do as he said, but her eyes spotted something just beyond her own reach.

"Uncle Alec! There's a knife over there. On the shelf. Maybe you could reach it!"

Alec followed her gaze to a little indentation in the wall just above the bunk, and with some pain, he struggled to shift his weight towards it. With his good arm he stretched as far as he possibly could. Another inch, a quarter of an inch…his fingers strained and reached until the knife was at last grasped between his fingers.

"I've got it," he said triumphantly. He twisted around and, with his hands still bound, began to use the blade to saw at the ropes binding Sara's wrists. "All right now, keep the rope taut."

Sara did as she was told, her spirits rising.

"Uncle Alec," she said, suddenly remembering. "There's a hole in the floor." She uncovered it with her toe.

Outside, a fly buzzed around Leo's head and he awoke, swatting at the air, wildly. He sat up and listened. Things were too still, too silent.

"Isis!" he called sharply. "Isis, where are you?" He walked over to the cart and made sure the doors were securely locked.

Sara was wriggling her hands out of the rope when they heard Leo's voice. She and Alec froze. Sara very slowly raised herself to look out the window.

"He's going!" she said excitedly. "He walked into the bush!" She immediately turned and started to untie Alec's hands.

"Don't, Sara. It'll waste time. You can get through that hole. Just go."

"No, we can make the hole bigger! Then you can fit! You can help me! He won't hear us! He's too far away!"

Alec looked at her and, realizing she was right, he kicked his feet at the hole with all his strength. He winced with pain, but with every kick another piece caved in, making it bigger.

Sara looked out the window and her heart froze. Leo had appeared at the edge of the bush and was heading towards the cart.

"He's coming back," she said.

Hetty swept the back porch furiously, scattering rose petals to the wind. Something at the edge of the garden caught her eye and she stepped back into the shadows. A figure was definitely hiding in the bushes. A woman with a shawl over her head came furtively across the yard and up the steps of the back porch, totally unaware of Hetty's presence. She crouched down and tried to push a letter under the door. Hetty grabbed a nearby bushel basket, jumped out, pulled it down over the woman's head and brought her to the ground, sitting on her.

"Olivia! Louisa!" she shrieked. "Help me!"

Louisa came running from the house with a broom and started hitting the unknown trespasser with it. Olivia, Janet and Felicity hovered behind her.

Hetty leaned down and talked to the bushel basket. "Stand up and face us, whoever you are!"

Louisa stood still, her broom poised, as the figure slowly drew herself up and removed the basket. It was Isis.

"Please, Ma'am," she said, "let me be! I know where they are. I can lead you to them."

Chapter Twenty

Alec made one last kick at the floorboards and a huge chunk splintered away, leaving a hole big enough to crawl through.

"Sara, listen to me! Go through there and run as fast as you can to the road."

"But what about you?" Sara stared at him and then frantically looked out the window at Leo's approaching form.

"I'll only slow you down," said Alec.

Sara persisted. "Maybe I can open the doors for you."

"Head down the hill, towards the main road. Don't worry about me. You just go and get some help!"

Sara rattled the doors to the cart, but they wouldn't budge. "I'm going to try to break the lock!"

"Sara, forget the lock and just get out of here before he comes back," shouted Alec.

Sara lowered herself through the hole. She climbed back up and kissed him on the cheek and then disappeared once again through the opening.

She crawled out from under the cart, breathing the fresh air deeply. She didn't care what Uncle Alec said, she was going to get him out of there. She rounded the corner, still hidden from Leo's view, and, picking up a rock, she tried to break the padlock on the door, hitting it over and over again.

"Sara, go on! Now!" She could hear her Uncle Alec yelling at her from inside. She realized that he was right, but it was too late. Leo had almost reached the door of the cart. She looked around madly for a place to hide. As she ducked out of sight, she spied a large box attached to the side of the cart. There was nothing else to do. She lifted the lid and jumped in, pulling the lid down after her. Something jabbed into her back uncomfortably, and from the stuffy darkness she could hear Leo's heavy tread on the stairs to the back doors of the cart. The key scraped in the lock and the doors squeaked open.

Sara lifted the lid of the box and crept out. Just as she was about to lower the lid back down, she noticed that it was half-filled with containers labeled "Concussion Powder." That's what had been sticking into her in the box, she thought. They were the same type of containers she had seen in the tent.

"Where is she?" Leo's voice bellowed at Alec, inside the cart.

Alec stared impassively up at the man's red face. Leo's eyes were bulging in anger; a vein throbbed in his forehead as he inspected the hole in the floorboards. He gripped his shotgun with white knuckles.

"She's long gone, Leo," said Alec. "You'll never catch her now."

The man grunted in anger.

"You should turn yourself in before this goes too far," Alec continued.

"Shut up!" Leo roared. He turned to leave. Alec tried to stall him, knowing that Sara had certainly not had enough time to escape.

"Leo! Wait!" he called.

Leo turned around.

"I, uh…I can help you escape," said Alec. "If you go looking for her, you'll just make it easier for them to find you."

Leo considered this, but then he shook his head and made for the door.

"You've got to realize that everyone's out there looking for Sara. Constable Jeffries and his men will be here at any moment."

Leo glared at Alec and fingered the trigger of his shotgun. "Next shot won't just graze you," he threatened.

Outside, crouched at the side of the cart, Sara could hear everything. She knew she should run, follow her Uncle Alec's directions down the hill to the main road, but her eyes were fastened on those containers. She knew they were the source of the smoke and the light she had witnessed inside that tent. She had seen Leo burn his hand when he had upset one accidentally. She quickly and carefully set some of the concussion-powder containers around the door of the cart, and, putting some more in her pockets, she climbed up to the driver's seat. From there, she pulled herself up to the top of the cart.

"Leo! Oh Leo!" she called softly.

Inside the cart, Leo stopped in his tracks and listened.

"Leo! Leo! Help me!" came the call again. Alec buried his face in his hands and shook his head.

Leo slowly and cautiously made his way to the doors of the cart. He threw them open and raised his gun, looking for the source of the voice. He knew she was out there somewhere.

Sara watched him from the roof of the cart, her heart pounding. She felt a small thrill of anticipation as Leo's foot headed straight for one of the tins of concussion powder.

"Leo! Help me!" she called very softly.

BANG!!! Leo had jumped from the cart and landed with both feet on two of the containers. Blue-and-green smoke poured from them as he leapt up and down holding on to his burned feet, howling with rage. It seemed every time he put his foot down he stepped on yet another tin of the explosive concoction that went off with the racket of gunpowder.

From the top of the cart, a beaming Sara, her eyes sparkling with delight, threw more tins at him. The din was indescribable. Leo waved his arms wildly and ran towards the bushes yelling, his feet burning, green, pink and blue smoke enveloping him. Sara jumped nimbly down to the driver's seat and down to the ground, carefully avoiding any remaining tins of powder. She headed for the cart doors.

Alec was straining to look out the window when Sara leapt into the cart.

"Sara! What the devil is going on? I told you to..."

Sara grabbed the knife and started cutting the ropes on his hands. "We have to hurry! He'll be back soon!" she said, as Alec's hands were freed and they both fumbled with the rope that bound his legs.

Leo was indeed coming back. He lurched and hobbled towards the door of the cart, muttering oaths.

"Rotten kid! I'll show her a thing or two..."

But Sara was ready for him. She grabbed a

heavy iron frying pan from the wall of the cart and jumped up on the bunk. Just as Leo's huge head appeared in the doorway, the frying pan came down on it, hard.

Leo looked stunned for a moment, an expression of pure disbelief on his face. Then his eyes closed and he fell backwards out of the cart, landing heavily on the ground, unconscious.

Sara helped an equally stunned Alec to the door and supported him as they climbed out of the cart, stepping over Leo.

Outside the cart at last, her Uncle Alec by her side, Sara emptied her pockets and threw the remaining concussion powder containers at the cart. To both their amazement, they instantly ignited the tins that were stored in the box. A chain reaction of brilliant blue, green and pink explosions began, sounding like a dozen guns.

Leo came to with a look of horror and stumbled and limped away from the cart, right into the arms of Abner Jeffries and a group of his men!

Two buggies careened into the clearing. Sara watched with her mouth open as Hetty, Olivia and Nanny Louisa jumped from one of them. They stood still for a moment, stunned, hardly believing what they were witnessing. Then Hetty spotted Sara and Alec, and she and

Louisa started running to them. From the other buggy came Janet, Andrew, Felicity and Felix.

Sara stared in disbelief—Isis was with them!

"Sara! Oh, Sara..." Hetty was laughing and crying at the same time as she ran across the clearing.

Tears of relief started rolling down Sara's cheeks as well, and the next thing she knew she was surrounded and being hugged by a dozen arms.

Alec was gathered to his brood as well, Janet bursting into fresh tears on seeing his wound. He assured her it was just a scratch, but in everyone's eyes he was a hero, and rightly so.

Nanny Louisa held Sara to her. "My Sara. Oh, my darling." Then she stood back in her best nanny fashion. "You wretched girl," she scolded. "We were so worried." Her face broke into a smile, however, and the tears rolled down her cheeks as she hugged Sara again.

Felicity and Felix stood there stunned, watching the fireworks as the rest of the concussion powder exploded.

"Sara sure knows how to put on a good show," said Felix. "This is even better than the one we started at Lawson's."

The minute he uttered the words, he knew he was in trouble. A sudden silence descended on the little group, and Alec turned and looked his son right in the eye. "We?" he said slowly.

Felix looked down at his feet, suddenly very interested in what he saw there.

His father continued. "I should have known you had something to do with that matter! We'll have to talk about this later."

Felix gulped and knew that the fireworks that were going off around him were nothing compared to the fireworks he faced at home.

Chapter Twenty-one

Sara sat in the parlor of Rose Cottage feeling very safe and secure, surrounded by her family. She quite enjoyed the role of the heroine. Alec sat holding Janet's hand, his arm still in a sling from his wound. Dr. Blair had called it more than just a scratch, but it was on the mend, and he too was enjoying the attention a hero deserves.

Olivia came over to Sara. Smiling at her fondly, she sat down and put a protective arm around her. Cecily claimed her other hand. Louisa J. Banks sat off to one side and simply observed. It was obvious to her the depth of warmth that existed between the King family and Sara. Her eyes filled, and at that moment she came to one of the hardest decisions she had ever made in her life. She dragged her mind back to the present, however, as Abner Jeffries cleared his throat and continued to read from the newspaper.

"'So, thanks to Constable Abner Jeffries of Avonlea... '" He cleared his throat again, and Sara could have sworn she saw the man blush before he went on. "'...and the Charlottetown police, the culprit, wanted in connection with several offences, is now behind bars.'" He looked up. "And I'll bet if anyone read his fortune, they'd see that he'd be there for a long, long time." He laughed appreciatively at his own joke, and then, when no one else in the room responded, he frowned and went back to reading. "'His accomplice was acquitted due to her cooperation in the case.'" He folded the newspaper and set it down with a flourish, looking as pleased as punch.

"Thank you, Abner. We appreciate you letting us know," said Alec, with a note of finality that intimated that perhaps it was time the constable moved on.

"Glad to be of service," said Abner, almost clicking his heels. Sara hid a smile. "I guess I'll be going then."

"I'll show you out, Abner," said Olivia graciously, and she led him to the front hall.

"Good day," Alec called after him, shaking his head with a grin. Janet squeezed his shoulder affectionately, not noticing Alec's sudden wince.

Felicity came over and took Olivia's place next to Sara. She smiled at her and held her hand. Sara smiled back.

"Oh, yes, Sara, I meant to tell you," began Alec, leaning forward in his chair. "Now that the fireworks season is over, Mr. Lawson says he thinks he could trust you to look after his store again...if you want to." His eyes twinkled.

Janet looked from Sara to Nanny Louisa and nudged him. "Alec!" she whispered, warningly.

Sara looked down at her lap, her face clouding suddenly. She glanced over at her Nanny Louisa.

"Oh...well, I don't really know...because it really depends on...whether I'm staying or not."

"Oh, Sara! You've got to!" Felicity burst out.

"Yeah. Don't leave," said Felix gruffly. "What will we do for excitement?"

Sara looked once again at her Nanny Louisa.

Louisa peered at her over the top of her wire-rimmed glasses. "Well, perhaps Sara would like to confer with her Aunt Hetty...?"

Janet looked around the room. "Where is Hetty?" she asked suddenly.

The sound of sobbing could be heard coming from the old wooden privy at the back of the garden behind Rose Cottage. Inside its gray and weathered walls stood Hetty King, the tears rolling down her cheeks, her shoulders shaking. She had come out here because she needed a place to be alone. Under no circumstances could she let the rest of her family see her in such a state. Now that the ordeal was all over, she felt quite undone in a way that truly surprised her. Another fresh wave of emotion washed over her, but she was cut off in mid-sob.

"Hetty?" came the call drifting across the backyard.

Hetty started. It was Louisa's voice. Of all people!

Frantically, Hetty wiped her eyes on her soggy hankie and attempted to compose herself. She straightened her blouse, tucked the hankie neatly away and made a last gesture to rub away the remaining evidence of tears. Then she tried the door. It wouldn't budge. She shook it. She rattled it. She pounded on it.

The racket could be heard all the way to the

Rose Cottage kitchen, and a small smile formed on Nanny Louisa's face. She went out the kitchen door and walked slowly across the lawn to the privy, which by now was fairly rocking back and forth with its occupant's agitation. Louisa smiled again as she looked at the outside hook, which had fallen neatly into the eye.

"Well, well, well," Louisa said quietly through the wooden slats of the door. "What kind of fool, I wonder, would go and get themselves locked inside a privy?"

There was an immediate silence. Then, after a long pause, came Hetty's voice.

"An old fool, I suppose." There was another silence. "Perhaps you were right about our need to modernize..." said Hetty, haltingly.

Inside, the poor woman wiped her eyes unsuccessfully as the tears started again, unbidden. "Time marches on. Things change..." Her voice broke.

· Louisa listened quietly, not finding it within herself to smile anymore. Behind her, Sara came out of the kitchen door looking for Hetty. She stopped when she saw the strange tableau. Her Nanny Louisa was talking to the privy! But then she heard Hetty's voice. She drew closer and listened.

"I presume you'll be taking Sara back to Montreal right away," Hetty was saying, her voice constricted.

Louisa was silent.

"I know you think," Hetty went on, "and rightly so, after all this, that she is safer in your care. And Sara probably can't wait to leave the Island after such a terrible experience. But it was my hope that she would want to stay in Avonlea. We'll miss her, you see. She belongs here...with her family."

Hetty started to sob. Sara listened gravely and lowered her eyes. So this was what her Aunt Hetty really felt. Her eyes brimmed with tears. A feeling of great relief filled her.

Olivia and Janet, followed by Alec, Felicity, Cecily, Andrew and Felix, trailed out onto the porch. Nanny Louisa turned to Sara and smiled, aware that she had been listening.

"I agree with you entirely, Hetty King," she said.

There was a moment of silence.

"What did you say?" Hetty finally said, staring at the wooden door, not quite believing what she had heard.

Outside, Nanny Louisa unhooked the door. Hetty came out of the privy, wiping her eyes. She stared at Louisa, who nodded, as if to confirm what she had just said. She looked at Sara, startled that she had obviously heard everything. Then she looked at the crowd on the porch. Oh, good Lord, she thought to herself. But her moment of embarrassment was brief, because Sara ran across the lawn and threw herself into her aunt's arms.

Nanny Louisa stood back and watched them.

"I don't think you'll be lonely very often, Sara, surrounded by such a caring family," she said.

Sara looked up and smiled at the crowd of people on the porch. *Her* family. The pain of losing her father was still sharp, but she hadn't lost everything. She still had her family. A sudden thought passed through her mind— what about Nanny Louisa? What would she do?

Nanny Louisa came over and joined in a three-way hug with Hetty and Sara. "Don't you worry about a thing at home," she said, almost as if she could read Sara's mind. "It'll do me good to take charge of things there. And then you can come and visit in a few months."

Sara smiled at the two women who held her so tightly. "Aunt Hetty will invite you to come visit us, too, won't you, Aunt Hetty?"

Hetty swallowed hard, and it wouldn't be truthful to say that her smile wasn't just slightly forced.

Louisa J. Banks looked at her old adversary with a twinkle in her eye.

"And I might accept," she said briskly. "*If* she keeps her promise and updates the facilities!"

She held her head high and glared over her glasses at Hetty, who smiled at her naturally and openly for the first time.

Sara laughed and grabbed her Aunt Hetty and her Nanny Louisa and dragged them towards the group on the veranda at Rose Cottage.

Peter Craig watched from the door of the woodshed. He looked up at the clear blue sky and sucked on a sweet piece of straw. Maybe now things would get back to normal. Summer stretched ahead, and he was sure its warmth would go a long way to help Sara through the days to come.